Messenger from the
Summer of Love

David Echt

Robert D. Reed Publishers
750 La Playa Street, Suite 647
San Francisco, CA 94121
Phone: 650/994-6570 • Fax: -6579
E-mail: 4bobreed@msn.com
http://www.rdrpublishers.com

Text Designer: Marilyn Yasmine Nadel
Editor: Jasmine Cori and Una Merrill
Cover Designer: Tom Skelly

David Echt's web-site:
http://themessenger.hipplanet.com/#David

ISBN 1885003757
Library of Congress Card Number: 00-109041

Produced and Printed in the United States of America

To the late Dr. Frederick Lenz
who was for many years
a powerful presence in my life and
continues to be an inspiration to me.

To the Venerable Hyunoog Sunim for
being an inspiration and example
through his own awakening.

To Adi Da Avabhasa for
his eternal Light and Love.

To anyone who ever wished upon a star...

Contents

Introduction

It's been over thirty years now since that fateful summer, The Summer of Love. Like everyone else who lived through that time, my life has gone on. The extraordinary events I witnessed then, seem almost like a dream. I never expected anyone to believe me, so for over thirty years I've maintained my silence.

After years of wandering from place to place, I finally settled in Boulder Colorado, at the foot of the Rocky Mountains. I've lived all over the country and traveled from coast to coast, from New York to Los Angeles, always anxious of talking about what I know of the past and what I know about a possible future. A day hasn't gone by that I haven't thought about it. And now those of my generation are growing older, and we need to pass on a legacy. I don't want time to forget how we dared to love.

It's in the shade of these majestic Rocky Mountains that I've found the silence to write.

Once a year, the town of Boulder celebrates the coming of summer with the Boulder Creek Festival. It's a huge outdoor event set along the lush, tree-lined Boulder Creek. It's clearly the biggest event of the year, and the whole town turns out for it. This year there were hundreds of booths with arts and crafts and plenty of great food and drink. There was an impressive array of ethnic dancing from all over the world but I came for the music and the spirit. It makes me a little nostalgic for that time in the sixties, but the feeling of unity that I so fondly reminisce is unfortunately gone. People are afraid now. Afraid to let their children play, afraid of how people will react if they smile at a stranger and afraid to be children. We've lost something precious. I fear we've become afraid to love. As I watched the crowds pushing past me, I wondered, what happened? What happened to the dream?

There were so many people at the festival that it was hard to walk through the crowd. I found myself having to weave my way around to avoid running into people. There were people pushing strollers, and some walking their dogs. And some not paying any attention at all and bumping into each other among the steady throngs. Although pleasant, it was chaotic and, at times, overwhelming. I stopped for a moment to get my perspective, and for just that moment, it looked like the crowd parted right before me.

Then I saw him.

The Master was standing right there. He looked radiant, bathed in golden light. He looked exactly as he did over thirty years ago: a young, handsome man, with curly blond hair and porcelain clear complexion. Ethereal yet very real at the same time. He hadn't aged a day since I last saw him. It felt as if time had stopped. There was a familiar stillness in the air that I remember from thirty years ago.

He looked right at me and smiled. A feeling of pure divine bliss enveloped my being; it felt as if it came from inside of me and from all around me at the same time. I was re-awakened by his presence. The Master once told me that what he does is awaken the light that's already there within you. I was too overwhelmed to move. It was like he had cleansed me of thirty years of residue from living on the Earth. I wanted to rush over to him, but as soon as that thought entered my mind, the crowd closed again, like the Red Sea. I looked all around, but he was gone. I knew I wouldn't find him. Once more, the crowd was a swarm of moving people going about their business. I could feel the warm sunlight against my skin and the sounds of talking and laughter returned to my ears, yet the blissful feeling of his emanation remained.

I walked over to a bench and sat down. I was in a state of utter amazement, yet sad because I couldn't find him. I put my head down in despair. Sitting right in front of my feet was a card maybe 4 x 6 inches in size. In large black print, it said, "It's time!"

A few weeks later I had a dream. In the dream, I was sitting on the white sandy banks of a desert river. It was warm and dry. I could see desert shrubs along the distance of the river. I looked over to my left, and the Master was sitting there. He looked at me with his eyes piercing my awareness and simply said, "It's time now."

I felt completely content sitting in the bliss of his presence. With a look of great compassion he said, "I want you to tell the world what happened." Then he reached out and gently touched my forehead between my eyebrows and just above, touching my third eye. I closed my eyes; from the point of his touch, I saw white light enter my body. It filled me with a gentle feeling of divine love. I awoke smiling.

I knew then what I had to do. I had to write this book. I immediately went down to my basement and found the old wooden chest where I kept all of my notes from thirty years earlier. I must have had a hundred old spiral-bound steno pads. It was a little like unearthing a time capsule. In addition to all of my original notes, I kept some other artifacts in the box: my old desert boots that I had painted in psychedelic colors, some beads I used to wear and a small round stone that the Master had once given me.

I felt it was time to sit down and meditate and let the light guide me to tell you the truth about the Summer of Love.

Chapter 1

The Soul's Journey

May 25th, 1967. Unexpectedly, I began rising up and away from my body. Gently at first, with the subtle presence of a brightness that seemed to be with me. Then, without effort, I began climbing higher and higher. The illumination that was all around me became increasingly brighter. The speed of my ascent accelerated. The light became ever brighter as I moved higher and higher. I flew at an astounding rate, faster than any plane could fly, and all the time the light kept increasing in intensity. I had never seen anything that bright before. Yet, it didn't hurt me in any way. I was fully conscious and awake in the dream yet I was unable to think. I was without the ability to even construct a thought. I was moving without any effort toward the light. The light had no center or outer boundary; it seemed to be everywhere.

In an instant, a thought emerged into my awareness, like a bubble rising from a pool of still water. It wasn't even a thought; it was an impulse, almost a feeling. I was afraid. It was that deep sort of fear, like when something jumps out at you from the dark. There's no time to think—just primal fear. My reaction was very much like that. Maybe it was fear of the unknown.

The next thing I remembered was waking up, but I knew I hadn't been dreaming. I was conscious yet in a dreamlike state the entire time. I opened my eyes and looked around. I saw the knotty wood frame of my cottage and the tie-dyed sheet that I used for a bedroom door. I was there in the safety of my cottage. I could hear the creek across the road through the bedroom window, and I felt the reassuring warmth and comfort of my bed.

I sat up slightly, carefully resting on one shoulder, trying not to make any noise. I wanted to tell Laura about what had just happened, but I didn't want to wake her. She looked so beautiful in her restful slumber. I looked at her with her long hair so shiny, like silk, her face the image of perfection. With her light, clear complexion and naturally dark eyelashes, she didn't need any makeup; she could turn heads just by walking into a room. I was in love with her.

A cool, spring breeze blew through the open window, pushing one of the shutters closed. She stirred, drew a deep breath, and slowly opened her deep blue eyes. She looked disoriented, as if she didn't know where she was. Laura looked at me incredulously. "Where am I?" she demanded, for a moment she seemed half asleep. I think she thought I was a character in her dream.

"You're at my place, Babe!"

She shook her head and said, "Wow, that was really weird. I was dreaming when something woke me up." Then she turned on her side, facing me. She pushed her hair back over her shoulder and said, "I dreamt that you had moved away. When I realized you were really gone, I tried to find you, but it was too late. I was here at your place, and all of your stuff was gone. Then I was somewhere else. I remember asking, Where am I?"

"I'm not going anywhere! Are you kidding? I love this place. I'd be crazy to leave. Besides, I could never leave you." Laura just looked at me and didn't say anything. I couldn't tell what she was thinking, as I usually could. So I changed the subject. "I had a really weird dream too. Or at least, I think it was a dream."

I described to her what happened, in as much detail as possible, but she seemed distracted. When I finished, she just looked away and said, "It sounds like you've been hanging out with that guy, you know, that guy who's always got a joint or two with him."

"You must be talking about Ernie."

"Yeah, him. What do you see in that guy? I don't want to be judgmental, but doesn't he seem like a loser to you?"

"Well, Ernie is with Ellen, Ellen and I have been good friends for a long time."

She sounded annoyed. "I don't know what she sees in him. I mean, Ellen seems kind of normal, and he's such a loser."

"Sometimes I wonder myself," I replied wistfully.

As usual, Laura had to rush off to do something that was more important than being right here with me. I wanted to be that something, someday. I wanted to feel like I was important too.

She drove off quickly and I was left alone to think about what had happened. I didn't have a clue if it was just a dream or something more. But I was about to find out that my life was going to change soon in a way I could never have imagined. What happened to me that summer had only happened to a few others. The experience I had in that dream was only a foreshadowing of the magic that was to come.

Chapter 2

Topanga Canyon

If you were to ask, I'd probably tell you that I was a typical American twenty-year-old living on my own. I owned a 65 VW microbus and I was delighted about my relationship with my girlfriend, Laura.

I was convinced that I had found the love of my life. I knew she was the one from the moment I first looked into her eyes. She was beautiful, smart, had a great sense of humor and she was a lot of fun to be with. We rarely had disagreements.

Working at home, I thought I had the coolest job in the world too. I was making silver jewelry and stringing beads that I sold locally to small head shops in Santa Monica and Hollywood. It all seemed perfect. For me, life couldn't have been better.

I found this cute, little cottage a few miles up Topanga Canyon. It was the kind of place where you might expect to find a great artist or writer. I never saw them, but I was told that Jim Morrison and Joni Mitchell were some of my neighbors.

Sitting in the middle of four acres, it was on a quiet little side street. In the evenings, I would be lulled to sleep by a seasonal stream trickling across the street. It was all very private.

There were places on the outer walls where the paint was worn away from years of weathering. It looked like it was built before there was electricity. In some places, I could see the pipe-like electrical conduit carrying the wiring throughout the house. Inside it was just nailed on the top of the wood paneling like it had been tacked on some years after the house was built. I thought this just added to the antique charm. It reminded me of a mountain cabin. It was my comfort home. It always gave me the feeling that everything was going to be OK. Reminiscent of a feeling I remembered as a child, lying in my mothers lap while she read to me.

My landlord was a retired movie "extra". He'd worked in a lot of old cowboy movies back in the early days of film. He was in some silent movies and later in the thirties he was featured in several talkies. He told me that he bought the cottage because they used to film in the area, and he needed a place to stay when they were working on location. Back then it must have taken a while to get there from Hollywood. I could easily imagine them, in their Model-T's, driving through the valley on dusty dirt roads. He told me how a lot of famous people from that time like Harry Carey and Bronco Billy would come over and hang-out with him in the evenings. I would often see a twinkle in his eye when he was recounting his good ol' days of Hollywood.

I had the feeling that he didn't care much about money. I don't think he'd changed the rent in over twenty years. He seemed more interested in renting to someone who would take care of his place. I was sure he didn't know what current rates were. My rent was an unbelievable three hundred dollars a month, so I wasn't about to leave anytime soon.

On the evenings when Laura couldn't come over, I would listen to the radio or write. I always kept a steno pad with me for that purpose. Living without a TV, I spent a lot of time keeping a journal of what I thought was important or interesting, or sometimes I would just write poetry. Most of it wasn't worth much, but I felt compelled to do it. Maybe because my father always kept a small notebook with him, and he would often stop whatever he was doing to write some important idea that popped into his head. It was part of his work as a screen writer. He convinced me at an early age to do the same. I wanted to be like him, so as a young child I would carry around a pad and paper and draw pictures. As I got older, I started writing. He would always tell me, "You never know who you're going to meet in this life. So write everything." He convinced me that something might come of my writing. So I inherited his compulsion. I wrote everything that happened, no matter how trivial.

California didn't get any better than living in the coastal mountains. I loved the scent of the native sage and chaparral that fills the air with their intoxicating fragrance. The Indians would burn the sage in ceremonies to purify the vibrations.

Behind the cabin there was an old shed that I rebuilt into a sauna. I took an old wood stove that I found at a flea market and pilled some stones around it, along with tin trays for water. A large stack of old weathered firewood sat along side the house, that was perfect for burning in the sauna.

Fog from the ocean would roll through the canyon, bringing cold air with it. It was that California kind of cold, where fifty degrees feels like it's only thirty. I looked forward to those chilly evenings.

Often friends would drop over for a sauna and friendly get-together. They would usually stay for hours and we'd talk and laugh the night away. When it got too hot in the sauna, we could just ramble outside and look at the stars while our bodies cooled off. My friends would bring their friends along and usually an offering of good wine and smoke, and we'd make a night of it. I was always meeting new people this way and expanding my circle of friends.

My favorite visitor was Sam. He was this adventurous guy that would stop by whenever he was in town. Sam was soft spoken and gentle by nature, but not shy. He had a lot of energy. I think it was hard for him to stay in any one place for too long.

Sam and I always had great conversations. He always looked beyond the topic to a deeper meaning. I think he was really searching for something.

It was near sunset and I was outside preparing the sauna when I saw Sam walking my way with his trademark buckskin coat and Australian bush hat. It was his style to stand out in a crowd.

"Hey man, it's good to see you!" I said. We gave each other a big hug. "I've got some friends coming over for a sauna in a few minutes. Are you going to stick around? How long are you going to be in L.A.?"

"Yeah Man, sounds cool! To answer your other question; I'm not staying, in the area too long. I just came to L.A. to get my shit. I'm moving up to San Francisco." He pulled off his hat and brushed his stringy long blond hair from his brow. "I was just there a few days ago."

I interrupted him before he could finish his sentence. "Help me carry some of these logs over for the fire. Ernie and Ellen and some other chick are coming over. Do you remember Ernie? I think he was over the last time you were here."

"Oh yeah, I remember him. He's cool." He picked up his previous train of thought. "Look, this chick I've been staying with is really pissed off right now because I'm leaving. I'm going by tomorrow to get my shit. She should be at work all day, so I won't have to deal with her."

I went inside the sauna to put the wood down. I placed a few logs in a neat stack in the corner of the shed where I could reach them in a hurry and keep the fire burning. Sam was still outside. "You aren't even going to talk to her?" I called out.

I looked back and saw Sam shake his head and put his hands up as if he was pushing something away. "No man, I just need to get away. Yesterday, when I told her over the phone, she got really ugly!"

I walked over to the faucet on the side of the shed. It was an old faucet that was sticking out of the dirt like it grew there. I filled up the bucket with water for the sauna. "How's she going to pay the rent? I mean, you can't just leave her like that."

"She was always the one paying the rent anyway. Shit, she's got a job at a bank!" Sam looked down and changed the subject. "How's um, um.. that chick you've been seeing?"

"You mean Laura?" I asked, as if it could have been anybody else.

"Yeah, Laura, I couldn't remember her name. I only met her that one time. You know, at that party, last year, down in Venice. All I remember was that she was really beautiful." He looked off in the distance like he was remembering something and murmured, "I was really fucked up that night."

I ignored his last statement. I was also remembering that night. "Do you remember that poet? Jim something? He was reciting this really eerie, haunting poetry that he wrote. He said he was going out to the desert, with his band, to take acid. He was really into his music." I paused, looking away and putting my hands deep in my pockets. "He asked us if we wanted to come with him to the desert, but I'm too freaked out about taking acid. I've heard some really weird stories about it. You know, people jumping out of windows and shit. Have you ever done anything like that?"

"I never jumped out a window but I took some powerful medicine once, in New Mexico, but it wasn't acid. I met this medicine man who gave me this thing that grows on a cactus. It's called peyote."

"I've never heard of it."

"It looks like a dry mushroom. I had to chew it and swallow it. It was really bitter, man. It tasted like puke. But after about an hour, I got really high."

"Is it like pot?"

"No man, it's really different." Sam's eyes rolled back as he tried to put the feeling into his words, "It's like gliding on air. You understand things about life. Everything's clear for a while. Until you come down."

"Hey, do you remember that chick, Grace?"

I had only met her once, but I remembered her because she was so unique. She wasn't like anyone I'd expect to see Sam with. She looked really preppie.

"Yeah, I remember her. She was beautiful. Wasn't she one of those Rose Parade queens or something? Where did you meet her?"

"I don't remember. But I talked to her a few weeks ago. I don't know why, but I just called her out of the blue. She told me that she was leaving everything behind because she had transcended."

"What? What is transcended? What was she talking about?"

"It's really weird, man. She just said that she knew that everything was God, and she didn't need anything material anymore. She even wrote her parents a letter and told them that she's transcended."

I heard Ernie's VW Van pull up. The engines in those vans make a very distinct sound. Plus you can recognize them by the sound of the doors when they close. They don't sound as "solid" as in American cars.

Soon Ernie, Ellen, and their friend came walking around the house. Ernie is a tall guy, about six foot two. He carries a pot belly, a friendly round face and a big, happy-looking mustache. He had a large, brown shopping bag in his arms.

"Hey, I got munchies!" he said, greeting me with a big, one-arm hug.

"How the hell are you? And who's your friend?" I asked.

Good Ol' Ernie, confused by the two questions at once, stuttered for a moment. "Uh, uh, this is Silvia. She just moved here from Chicago." I couldn't help but notice how cute she was. Long, straight blond hair, clear blue eyes, and a smile that could light up a room.

"Hi, I'm Trevor, and this is my friend, Sam." I started to put out my hand to greet her, but her eyes were clearly looking up at Sam.

Sam took off his hat, letting his long locks fall down on his shoulders. He stepped up to introduce himself. "Hi, I'm Sam."

She took his hand. "My name is Silvia."

He uttered her name softly while Silvia looked down at her toes, slightly embarrassed she said. "It's my great aunt's name, so I got stuck with it. I want to change it." She looked up shyly and gazed into his eyes. Suddenly, there was a silence that was uncomfortable to everyone but the two of them.

Ernie, oblivious, yelled out, "Hey I've got to put this stuff in the fridge!"

I returned to playing the host. "The door's open, man. Help yourself."

Sam and Silvia were still lost in their own world. Ellen looked at me and smiled. Her voice was slightly raspy, and she told me that she was getting over a cold. She quietly asked "Do you want a beer?"

"Sure."

I looked back and saw Sam and Silvia talking as if they had known each other for years. It was around sunset and getting a little chilly, so I went over to the sauna to get the fire started. Everyone congregated around these two benches I had placed just outside the sauna. The firewood was dry, so it didn't take much to get it started. I lit some candles and turned out the light.

Ernie yelled, "How's it going in there?."

I stepped outside the door and motioned to come in. "It's ready. Come on in." It was almost dark, and I think the twilight helped to hide peoples' self-consciousness about getting undressed in front of each other. I did notice that while Sam was taking off his trousers, Silvia snuck a peek, and then quickly looked down, grinning slightly. I also caught Sam taking a long, lingering look at her as she pulled her dress over her head. He couldn't contain his grin. As Silvia let the dress slip from her hand and fall gracefully to the ground, she closed her eyes and leaned her head back slightly, shaking her hair and running her fingers through it like a comb. I couldn't help but think that she knew he was watching. The sauna door had a spring that kept it shut, so I stood there holding it open for everyone to come in.

Ernie was the first one in the door. "It feels great in here!" he exclaimed, while finding a comfortable place to sit. Silvia looked at

Sam and saw that he had been watching her. They paused for a moment then simultaneously giggled. "I'm not holdin' this door all night," I grumbled, trying to break the ice. They both laughed and filed in past me.

Ellen came skipping from the house caring the bag of treats. Her long, dark hair bounced as she skipped. I was always taken by her big, beautiful eyes and her slightly olive complexion. She told me once that she was part Cherokee, although she really didn't look like it. I think it was her great, great, great grandmother. "You don't have to wait for me," she said as she put the bag down on one of the benches and quickly slipped her clothes off. She grabbed the bag and filed past me. "Oh, this feels great! It's getting cold out there!" Ellen said with a quiver in her voice.

I shut the door to the chilly night and said... "Scoot over Ellen. I need to sit by the fire, so I can keep the stove going." The room was small, so we were all sitting pretty close together. I was rubbing against Ellen's thigh. Ellen had long been like a sister to me. I'm not sure when or even where we met, but we'd known each other for years. I always felt comfortable being around her. I knew I could trust her. Sometimes she would be my confidant and we'd talk about things that we were happening in our personal lives.

We heard the sound of a can pop open and Ernie's voice. "Anybody want one?"

Feeling in a festive mood Sam was the first to volunteer. "Sure."

Silvia was pretty, but she looked a little inexperienced socially. She jumped in, like she was trying to compensate, saying, "Yeah, me too."

"Are they cold?" I asked. I hated warm beer.

Ernie always put himself in charge of the party treats. "I put them in the freezer when we got here, just for you, man."He took a sip. "They're just right."

I decided to try one, even though I wasn't much of a drinker.

"Ernie, I've already got one," Ellen snapped. Turning to Sam, she sweetly asked, "Are you from around here?"

I dipped my hand in one of the pails of water, scooped up a handful and tossed it at the stove. It made this great hissing sound, and a cloud of steam billowed into the air.

"Well I'm kinda from nowhere right now. I mean, I'm moving."

I think he didn't want Silvia to know his situation. Silvia looked a little disappointed. "Moving where?" she asked.

"I'm going to San Francisco. You see, San Francisco's where it's at right now." He was looking only at Silvia. Then he looked at the rest of us. "I was just there a few days ago. You gotta see what's happening to believe it."

"Isn't it really cold up there?" Ernie asked. He made a motion like he was shivering. Ernie didn't like discomfort. He was happiest with a cold beer or a joint in his hand.

"I've never been there," I added.

"There's something really happening up there," Sam said enthusiastically. "It's like everything is free. I met these people who lived in a big house on Page Street, not too far from Golden Gate Park. I don't know whose house it was. A lot of hippies were crashing there. It's like everyone was family. No, it was better than that. My family was always fighting."

"I usually try to stay away from my family," Ernie said. "They don't understand me. Shit! I don't even understand me."

"So, when are you leaving?" Silvia asked.

"I don't know," Sam looking down answered quickly.

I wanted to know more about this place. "Do you mean it's like being with your family?"

Sam looked a little annoyed at the question. "It's not that kind of family, man." Then he looked at Silvia. "I don't know when I'm going. I don't exactly have anywhere else to go right now. I'm kinda in transition."

I think it was obvious to all of us that Silvia was becoming quite interested in Sam. "What do you mean?"

Sam turned to me and asked, "Trevor, Is it OK if I crash here tonight?" People crashed at my place all the time, so I said, "Sure, man. You can use the living room. That couch opens out to a double bed and it's real comfortable. If you open the window, you can hear the creek across the street. It'll put you right to sleep."

"Thanks man, that sounds great!"

Ellen looked over at me. "Hey Trevor, where's Laura? We never see her anymore. Are you guys still together?"

"Yeah, were still together," I answered, my voice dropping. I must have sounded a little disappointed. "She's just always busy with school. And her parents hate me. I can't even go over to her house anymore. They want her to marry some establishment guy. You know, a doctor or lawyer. Someone with a haircut and a big house."

I hadn't had a haircut in about a year. I know Laura's parents saw me as a loser. The last time I was over there, her dad wouldn't even speak to me. He just mumbled something under his breath and walked away. I didn't want to go to school, and I didn't have a real job. It seemed like they expected more from me than my own parents did. My folks never hassled me. I felt like they really knew how to love unconditionally. I couldn't understand why Laura let her family run her life.

Sam mumbled, "That's a bummer, man."

Ellen was more sympathetic. "Is that why she's not here? Is she afraid of her parents?"

I know my voice was mopey, "I brought her to this family get-together last month. It was my parents' twenty-fifth anniversary. She met all of my rich cousins and all of my "war hero" uncles. They were quite a show. It made me feel like a real loser. Maybe that had something to do with it. I ended up getting into a big fight with my uncles."

"Shit, what happened?" Sam asked.

"We started talking about the war, and my uncle Jack asked me if I was enlisting. I told him I wasn't going and I thought the war was immoral."

"Good for you." Ellen cheered. "I think you should stand up for what you believe in."

"Thank You!" I said while taking a bow.

"Well, I've got two uncles that fought in World War II, my mom has two cousins who fought in Korea, and two of my cousins are already in Viet Nam. They all think I'm some kind of coward."

"They don't know who you are," Ellen said, touching my knee.

"Thanks. Their kids, my cousins are all doing the right things. They are either going to school or carrying rifles in some rice paddy. At times, I thought Laura was actually impressed with those guys! I don't know where she's at sometimes! She thinks my cousins are, as she says, 'going somewhere.' And she lets her parents run her life! I don't get it!"

"She should just split, man," Sam muttered. It was like that for him. If things felt too restrictive, he'd just leave. I didn't know if he meant that she should leave me or her parents. He probably didn't even know. I never knew Sam to have any attachments.

Silvia added, "I did!" Even though I think her parents knew where she was. She was more likely just trying to impress Sam.

I tried to explain, although I think I was really trying to convince myself. "She's gotta stay until she finishes school. I don't know if she's afraid of her parents or not, but sometimes she seems a bit straight."

"Maybe you should split!" Sam joked.

"No I can't. I'm really into her."

"Do you love her?" Silvia asked. That made me a little mad because it seemed like she was looking for salacious details.

Ernie, in the meantime, had pulled something out of his bag and was trying to light a pipe. It looked like it was hand carved, and it had some feathers and beads hanging from its long stem.

Sam looked impressed with the pipe. "Wow, did you get that at Ralph's market?" We all laughed. "Really," Sam asked, studying the pipe. "Where'd you get it, man? It's beautiful!"

"I traded it for two lids, " Ernie answered, holding a lighter to the bowl. He puffed a few times to get the pipe started. Smoke quickly filled the tiny room. He took a big hit and then passed it on to Sam.

Sam was still studying the pipe. "Thanks, man."

"That's what friends are for," Ernie replied, his eyes slightly glazed.

I put another log in the fire and threw some more water on the stove. The room was filled with steam and smoke. Whenever a breeze blew through the cracks in the shed, the steam would swirl.

"This reminds me of New Mexico," Sam said, moving into his story mode.

Sylvia looked impressed. Personally, I think she would have been impressed with anything he said at that point. "I've never been there. What's it like?"

"I stayed in this little town called Taos."

"Tow-aus?" Silvia repeated, not sure how to pronounce it.

Sam laughed. "It's some kind of Indian name." He spelled it out, like in a spelling bee. "T-A-O-S, Taos.

There's a place there where Indians have been living for over a thousand years. They call it a pueblo."

"Like tepees?" I asked.

"No, these are buildings. Like mud apartments. It actually looks kinda like an apartment house."

Ernie emerged from his fog. "That sounds like my old place!"

"Did you stay there?" Ellen asked, ignoring Ernie.

"No, I stayed in this old adobe house a few miles out of town. It was about the same size as Trevor's pad, but it didn't have any running water."

Ellen shook her head. "I couldn't do that."

Ernie puffed away at the pipe. "Now that definitely sounds like my old apartment."

Sam continued. "There was a well, outside the house, with an old hand pump. I think it was over a hundred years old." Sam passed the pipe to Silvia.

"Wow!" was all Ernie said. It seemed like he was going to go on, but he never finished his sentence. I think he was starting to get high.

"So, what did you do there?" Silvia leaned forward and asked with great interest.

"Just lived. It was beautiful! I felt like a human being is supposed to feel. This chick I met introduced me to a medicine man."

Ernie held up his palm, like in an old cowboy movie. "How!"

I ignored Ernie too. "You know, I've never seen a medicine man, except in movies. Actually, what is a medicine man? What does he do? Is he like a doctor?"

"He's got some herbs for the body, but what he really does is heal the spirit. He's like a guide for the soul. While I was there, they let me be part of this sacred ceremony. They said I was the first white man they had ever invited."

Silvia looked very impressed. "Wow!"

"They had this room they had dug into the ground and there was a ladder to get down into it. Once you were inside, they would start a fire."

"Like this one?" I asked, as I tossed more water on the stove.

We had been passing the pipe around the circle, each taking a hit. Ernie looked at Ellen. "Do you wanna pass that down to me?" Startled, Ellen noticed the pipe in her hand. "Oh, sorry!"

Ernie filled the pipe again as Sam tried to explain. "Yeah, it was kinda like this, but it was sacred."

Silvia looked at him in awe. "What do you mean, sacred?"

"The kiva, that's what they call it, is used for religious ceremonies. It's a place where you get in touch with the spirits. You can go and pray for good weather or to heal an illness. In the old days, they'd ask for a successful hunt. Sometimes the warriors are down there for days without coming out. They wait for a vision to lead the tribe."

This piqued my curiosity. I had always been interested in things like this. "Did that happen to you? Did you have a vision?

"I can't tell you everything, but it was really powerful. I was there for only one evening. But at the end of it, the medicine man gave me a name."

"What name?" Silvia asked, looking mystified.

"He said, 'Night Cloud.'"

"That's really beautiful," Silvia murmured softly.

It was silent for a minute, and then Ellen said, "It's getting really hot in here. I'm going outside."

"That sounds like a good idea," I added, following Ellen out the door. Ernie just kept smoking as Sam and Silvia continued their conversation, lost in their own private world.

The fresh air felt good. It was cold out, but we couldn't feel it after being inside the sauna and absorbing so much heat. The moonlight was filtering through the trees, casting a bluish tint to the landscape. In the dim light, I could see steam rising off of our bodies.

"So what's been happening with you and Ernie lately?" I asked.

Ellen was pensive, looking out at some trees. "Oh, I started painting again. I really like it; I just wish I could do it for a living. I don't know, I'm sick of my job. I need to do something different, something more creative."

"What do you want to do?" I wanted to give her some encouragement. "I'm actually making a living doing jewelry. Maybe you could do something like that. You know, sell your art work." I'd seen Ellen's paintings before, and I knew she was an excellent artist. Her work has a soft, delicate look to it. Lots of castles, white clouds, and fair young maidens. I think she liked to escape through her art.

Ellen leaned over and whispered, "It's Ernie too! All he wants to do anymore is get stoned. He's lost any motivation he ever had. Not that he ever had much, but I can't reach him any more." She had leaned forward to whisper, and did not move back.

I was starting to feel self-conscious with her standing naked, so close to me. I had always thought Ellen was pretty, but I had never seen her in quite this way before. My attraction was making me feel slightly uncomfortable. "What if Ernie walked out here?"

"Well, what are you thinking of doing? I wanna be free like Sam. I think it's great the way he does whatever he wants to. You know the way he acts on every instinct." She looked me right in the eyes. Her face was no more than six inches away from mine. "Don't you?"

Shit! I didn't think I was that naïve. Why didn't I see this coming? And Ernie's a friend a mine. I had about a second to either kiss her and make our friendship really uncomfortable or do nothing and make our friendship really uncomfortable. I have to admit she looked lovely in the moonlight.

"So, what do you think?" Ellen whispered in her most inviting voice. She was so close that I could feel her breath as she spoke.

"I'm thinking!" I uttered foolishly, and we both burst out laughing.

Just at that moment, Sam and Silvia came out. "What's so funny?" Silvia wondered out loud.

"Oh, you had to have been there." Ellen answered.

Sam stretched his arms overhead."It's nice out here. You can see the moon and stars." He looked up at the night sky. "This guy in San Francisco did my astrology. He said my moon is in Sagittarius. That's supposed to mean I like to travel. He did a really good reading for me."

"I'm a Capricorn." I jumped in.

Still eager to change the subject from what we were laughing about, Ellen looked at me flirtatiously and said,"I'm an Aquarian. We're supposed to be free and open-minded."

"What are you, Silvia?" Sam asked eagerly.

She thought for a moment. "I don't know."

"Well, when is your birthday?" Sam asked.

"December seventh."

"Isn't that the day that Pearl Harbor was bombed?" I asked.

"Yeah, my parents had me to commemorate the holiday," Silvia snapped. She must have heard that one too many times.

Sam paused for a moment, thinking. "Oh, you're a Sagittarian."

"What's Ernie?" I asked Ellen.

Ellen lowered her voice. "He's stoned. I should go see how he's doing." Ellen opened the sauna door, and a puff of smoke came floating out.

We talked for a while, and then went back into the sauna where we talked and laughed for a few more hours. I think Ernie had either a beer or that pipe in his hand the entire evening. Finally Ellen looked over at Ernie, who was half conscious and said, "It's time for me to get this guy home."

"I guess I'm a little wasted," Ernie mumbled chuckling.

"So what's new?" Ellen asked, unable to hide the cynicism in her voice.

Sam and Silvia were quietly whispering to each other when the rest of us passed by on our way out the door. I think this was the first time Ernie had been outside the sauna all night. We sat down on the benches and got dressed.

As she was slipping her clothes back on, Ellen casually looked up at me and said, "I hope that I didn't freak you out earlier. I don't know, I've been going through something lately."

Ernie seemed oblivious to our conversation. I wanted to say something to let Ellen know that's I was OK with it, and that, above all else, I wanted to stay friends. "Look, if this had been some other time, who knows? But I think it's probably better this way."

Ellen looked as though she was about to say something, but then we heard Ernie starting to stumble over toward us. She stood up and grabbed Ernie's arm to steady him. She looked at me incredulously and asked, "Would you believe he has to go to work tomorrow?"

They hobbled toward their car. Then Ellen stopped and started laughing. "Shit! I almost forgot Silvia!"

I laughed because I had forgotten about her too.

Ellen leaned back towards the sauna door and called in, "Silvia? We're going now. Do you want to stay here tonight?" She looked at me and asked, "Is that OK?"

What could I say? "She and Sam are going to have to stay in the same room." We both laughed.

Silvia's voice came through the door. "OK!"

Then I heard Sam ask, "Is that alright, man?"

I raised my voice a little so they could hear me.   "I'll leave the door open, so you can come in whenever you want to."

"Thanks!" Sam answered. And then Silvia laughed.

Ellen and Ernie drove away, and I retired to the house. I felt relieved that things had worked out with Ellen. She was a hard temptation to resist, but I was very much in love with Laura, and I didn't want to complicate things. I had met Ellen several years before she and Ernie were living together, and I had always felt closer to her than to him. I just hoped we could still remain close friends without any kind of weird tension between us.

My house had some old furniture that I had picked up at a flea market. It may have been old and cheap, but it was comfortable. I suppose to most people it wasn't much to look at. I looked around the kitchen at the wood cabinets thick with the paint of the past fifty years and then down at the worn and cracked linoleum floor. I suppose it wasn't much, but it was my first place. I had picked up a chrome kitchen table with a red Formica top and worn chairs that matched. Someone had patched the chairs with tape where they had torn.

The bedroom was small and without a real door dividing it from the living room. I had an Indian tapestry and some strings of beads hanging in front of a tie-dyed cloth. It didn't really block out any sounds from the living room, but it looked really groovy. The bathroom had two doors, one that opened to the living room, and the other to the bedroom, so I didn't have to walk past anyone who was staying in the house. I had a hide-a-bed in the living room that I always kept made for guest; All I had to do was pull it out.

I kept a small lamp above my bed with a dim twenty-five watt bulb that I used for writing in the evenings. I liked the mood set by the dim lighting. I always wrote in my journal before going to sleep. I would usually lie in bed writing and would sometimes fall asleep with a pen still in my hand.

I was just climbing into bed for the evening, when I heard Sam and Silvia opening the back door. It made a distinctive creaking sound. I think the hinge needed oiling. It was impossible to not make that scratchy noise, no matter how hard you tried. They were both trying to be quiet, but it was a tiny house, and I could hear every footstep and almost every word that was being said. I think they deliberately came in late, hoping that I would already be asleep, so that they could be alone.

I could hear them whispering in the kitchen and ruffling a paper bag. I guess Ernie forgot his treats. I heard Sam whisper, "Let's see what's in the bag. Hey, here's a bottle of orange juice! That'll be good in the morning. He left some chips. Here's a box of crayons and.." He paused. "Check this out. It's, Mr. Bubble!" There was laughter, followed by a "Shhhh" sound.

"We don't want to wake Trevor up," Sylvia whispered.

"Oh yeah, I forgot. Are you hungry? I've still got the munchies. Let's check out the fridge."

"Are you sure this is OK?"

"I'll go to the store tomorrow."

People seldom did. It's that small loan, when a friend says, "Can I borrow a few bucks? I'll pay you back tomorrow." that you know you're never going to see it again. It shouldn't even be called a loan. I could hear things sliding around on the shelves of the refrigerator. "I just want some orange juice," Sylvia was saying.

I tried not to pay attention, so I started writing in my journal. I wrote every night. I don't know how I got started doing this. It began when I was a kid. Because my dad was a screenwriter, I think I wanted to be like him. Unlike most men of his generation, he didn't go off to work every day. Instead he went to his office and sat behind a typewriter, working on some screenplay. He kept a closet full of writing supplies, like pencils, erasers, and lots of steno pads that he'd use for his work. I could just go into his closet and help myself. Sometimes he'd put a little toy in there for me.

I was writing about Laura and wishing I could see her more often. I longed for the days when we first met. When I first got this place, she was over all the time. We'd cook meals, take saunas together, and dream about places we'd go or things we'd do some day. We were happy. I always assumed she'd move in with me at some point. Even though she usually could never spend the whole night, I would see her three or four times a week. I asked her to move in once, but she couldn't because of school. Her parents are paying for her education, her car, her spending money-they pay for everything! They owned her, and she didn't want to piss them off. She told me that she'd move out as soon as she graduates. But things have changed this past year. The amount of time we share has gradually eroded to two or maybe three nights a month. She's busy all the time now. I'm thinking that summer's around the corner, and we'll have more time together then.

Sam and Silvia moved into the living room, and their voices were really clear. It was hard not to listen.

"Where are you going to stay, when you get up there?" Silvia asked. I assume she was talking about Sam's upcoming San Francisco trip. I'd been kinda wondering about that.

"It doesn't matter," I heard Sam reply. "I can stay in the park there!"

"I've never been there. What park?"

"Have you ever been to New York?"

"A few times. But I was a kid. You know, on vacation with my parents."

"Did you see Central Park?"

"Yeah, it's real nice."

"Well there's a park in San Francisco called Golden Gate Park. It's kinda like Central Park in New York but a lot cleaner, and no muggers. Northern California is really beautiful. It's not like here."

Silvia sounded surprised. "What's wrong with here? This place is beautiful. You've obviously never been to Chicago."

Sam laughed quietly. "Yeah, I have. I had a good time there."

"Are you shitting me?"

"Yeah! It really was a bummer," Sam answered, and they both laughed. Then Sam said something that really surprised me. "Why don't you come with me to San Francisco?"

Silvia sounded surprised too considering the earlier discussion. "What's up there?"

With Sam, there was always a feeling of wanting to explore the unknown. He said, "I'm not sure! There's something in the air. People are free there. I want to be a part of it. I don't want to miss it. You've got to come with me!" He paused for a moment. "I saw a store there where everything was free! Can you believe it! This group called the Diggers, or something runs it. Everything was free! You can take what you need, or leave stuff that someone else might need. You're going to love it there! Just say you'll come."

Silvia seemed taken by surprise. "I don't know!" It was like she was thinking out loud. "I guess I don't have anything here. You know, I haven't even looked for a place to live. Shit! You're really something. I thought I knew exactly what I was going to do, and then you come along! I don't even know you. I don't even know your last name, yet I think I love you."

"I don't think I can live without you in my life," Sam said softly. "I've never met anyone like you. I felt something from the moment I laid eyes on you. It's like I've always known you. I've gotta go. I want you to be with me. I love you."

It sounded like they were kissing. All that I can say for sure is that they weren't talking. After a while Sam asked, "So, is that a yes?"

"Why not?" Silvia replied, resigned to her fate.

"Far out!"

"Shit! My family's gonna freak out." Suddenly remembering something, Sylvia said, "I'm supposed to stay with my cousin Ellen until I get settled. I've gotta see my aunt and uncle this weekend. Do you want to come?"

Sam didn't answer right away. Then he changed the subject "Hey, I thought of a name for you."

"What is it?" she asked with excitement.

Sam lowered his voice, as if he was certain. "Silver. What do you think? It's already kinda like your name now."

I heard sheets ruffling as Silvia quietly repeated the name, "Silver, Silver, Silver..." over and over.

"Do you like it?" Sam asked impatiently.

"Yeah! I wish I had thought of it myself." This seemed to reassure him. He sounded proud of himself. "OK, I'm going to call you Silver from now on."

"I need to get used to it," she said. "I always hated my name before. It sounds like an old lady."

"Your name is Silver now," he said, as if making some kind of proclamation. Then he shifted thoughts. "Do you have any wheels?"

"What?"

"You know wheels, a car?"

"Yeah, I've got a Falcon. I drove it here from Chicago."

"That's beautiful!" Sam said, sounding very happy. "Let's take it."

"So, what about this weekend?" Silver asked sounding con-

cerned. Even though I didn't really know her it was slightly jarring
to call her Silver in my mind.

"My aunt and uncle, they're expecting me."

This was totally predictable to me. I had never known Sam to put
himself out for anyone, and I couldn't imagine him starting now.

"Let's leave this weekend."

"But I can't! They're expecting me," she said in a pleading voice.

"Fuck that! Let's just go!" Sam was an impatient guy, and I know
he didn't want to see anyone's relatives. I don't think he even saw
his own family.

There was soft laughter, followed by muffled sounds of rustling
between the sheets. I never heard if she was going to go or not, but
I knew for sure that Sam was never going to meet her family. It just
wasn't in his nature.

I tried to refocus my attention on my notes. I was trying to
remember as many details as I could of the evening. Writing helps
me relax. Occasionally I would hear soft laughter from the other
room, but things were quieting down now. I could hear the creek
across the street again and feel the wind blowing gently through my
open window. My thoughts drifted to Laura as sleep took over,
Laura...

Chapter 3

Laura

I had tickets to see Bob Dylan at the Hollywood Bowl. It's an evening that I had been planning for over a month. We were going to be in the fifth row, center, and I was thrilled. I think Dylan was one of the defining artist of a generation.

The Hollywood bowl was built in the early twenties, a time when you might see the likes of Mary Pickford, Greta Garbo or Charlie Chaplin there to see a classical symphony. The outside of the theater has a beautiful Art Deco facade which gives it a feeling of old Hollywood elegance. A lot of the old buildings in the area were built in this same time when Deco was the style during the golden age of Hollywood. You can drive through parts of Hollywood and West Los Angeles and still see these classic old structures. Just past the facade is a large open amphitheater with rows of seating sloping upward, looking down at the bandshell. The theater sits in a lush ravine surrounded by large, shady trees. In the summer the scent of eucalyptus is inescapable. On a clear night you can look up and see a million stars shimmering overhead.

Since her dad forbade her from seeing me, I couldn't go to Laura's house. I had to pick her up at Northridge College in the valley, where she was going to school. I had arranged to meet her in the parking lot by the Arts building at six. Having arrived a few minutes early, I sat in my van and waited. I started fussing with the radio, trying to find something interesting to listen to. My favorite DJ, B. Mitchell Reed, was about to come on the air. I was busy turning the dial, looking for KFWB, when I looked up and saw Laura in the distance, walking towards me. She looked gorgeous with her long, black hair delicately curled at the ends. Her emerald green eyes and a clear porcelain complexion always got a second look from anyone who saw her. Her short, white gauze dress looked translucent in the sunlight; I could clearly see every beautiful curve of her body. Her dress had a white cotton macramé belt resting on her hips, and she was wearing a pair of Grecian sandals that laced up her calves. She looked like a goddess.

She looked at me and smiled ever so sweetly, then hopped in the van. "You're beautiful!" I said with reverence in my voice. Then I leaned over to kiss her. She met me half way. Her lips were warm and inviting. She always left me feeling like I wanted more.

"Thank you," she responded politely.

I started the engine and asked, "So, how's school? I know it's only been a few days, but I feel like I haven't seen you in weeks."

She responded in a flat tone. "I've been so busy; I don't have time to think anymore." She seemed a little annoyed. I don't know what it was, but she was acting different. She usually opened right up and would tell me what she's been doing.

I tried to be comforting. "Well, spring break is almost here." She gazed out the window with a pensive look. She seemed a thousand miles away. Trying to start some kind of conversation, I said, "I'm really excited about this concert." She sighed, and nodded her head slightly, but didn't respond. Then I thought of a way to change her mood. I opened my ashtray and took out a joint that I had sitting there.

Laura looked surprised. "Where did you get that?"

"Ernie was over the other day and left four of these in the sauna. You know Ernie, he'll never miss it."

"Why are you friends with that guy?" Laura asked with irritation in her voice. "Doesn't he bother you?"

I was a little taken by surprise; she had never acted like this before. I was starting to feel a little defensive. "Ernie's OK."

"Are you still having your little sauna parties?" She was actually starting to sound openly sarcastic.

"Well, you know, just with friends," I explained.

"So, which friends this time?"

It was kind of weird because I had been having these sauna get togethers for a long time. I was racking my brain trying to figure out what why she was hassled by it now. "Hey babe, what's wrong?" I asked, reaching over to touch her hand.

"Nothing's wrong," she said softly, stroking my hand for a minute. Then her eyes clouded over and she let go. The irritation rose in her voice again. "I just want to know who you have been receiving in your birthday suit."

"OK. Ernie, Ellen, and Sam dropped by and Ellen had a cousin with her." I talked carefully, like I was walking through a booby trap. I didn't want to set off any explosions before the concert. I was also trying to talk while driving down the 101, lighting a joint, and checking the mirror for cops, all at the same time. I kept thinking that maybe she would be cool if she just got a little weed in her. School must be bumming her out.

She sat there with her legs and arms sternly crossed. "So, who's this cousin? I'm assuming it is a girl."

I felt myself starting to feel defensive again, as she looked at me with a steely stare. "Yeah, that's right," I answered, trying to ignore her insinuation. "Her name is Silvia. She just moved here from Chicago."

"So, where's she living?"

"With Ellen and Ernie. Remember, it's Ellen's cousin?"

I finally got the joint lit and handed it to her. Laura took a hit. Then she looked out the window, suddenly aware that this was an illegal practice.

"Maybe we should wait until we get there. I think it would be a lot safer." Then she took a really big hit and handed it back to me.

I proceeded to tell her about the sauna, even saying that I thought Sam and Silvia had fallen in love. I deliberately edited out the part about my encounter with Ellen. I took a last hit from the joint and put it back in the ash tray.

The joint started to take effect finally, and Laura mellowed out. "What happened with them?" she asked dreamily.

"They never met before that night. It was great! From the moment they first saw each other, there was a spark. They didn't really fall in love—it's more like they were already in love." Now I had her attention.

"So, tell me. What happened?"

"They ended up spending the night."

"At your place? Where were you?"

"I was sleeping in the other room, or at least they thought I was sleeping."

She laughed. It was really good to hear her laughter. It made me feel more relaxed again.

"So, what did you hear?" she asked in a conspiratorial tone.

"Plenty!" At that, we both laughed. Inwardly, I was thankful to good ol' Ernie for leaving those joints. I told her more about the evening and as much as I could remember about Sam and Silvia. She seemed entranced by the story. "In the morning I had to take them back to Ernie and Ellen's. I talked to them in the morning and Silvia said she was just stopped by Ellen's to get her stuff and then they were leaving that very day for San Francisco."

"Do you mean they were going to live together, just like that!" Laura asked in an astonished tone. She looked off in the distance and under her breath she mumbled, "How romantic!"

I almost asked her what she meant. Then I thought about how her parents were paying for school. She couldn't just take off like that. I realized that it must be a drag to be so tied down. I hoped she would have a good time tonight.

We took the Highland exit into the Bowl and were guided by attendants to a parking spot. I made a point of trying to remember where the car was so we could find it on the way out. "The Oden lot, the Oden lot," I repeated to myself.

I loved the feeling in the air. It seemed somehow alive. There was a pretty big crowd forming and we followed them up to the theater. I noticed how excited everyone was.

It was a colorful and diverse crowd. I saw every kind of person imaginable. There was one group of guys dressed like they were a part of a fraternity. With their short hair, neatly pressed slacks and plaid shirts, they looked liked Wally from "Leave It To Beaver." Just behind them there was a couple not wearing much at all. The girl wore a string bikini top and a pair of shorts that hung low on her hips. She must have had a dozen strings of beads hanging around her neck. The guy just had on a leather loin cloth, you know, like Tarzan, and was carrying a staff. Of course, he had beads, and a matching headband. Practically everyone was wearing beads. I had on a pair or bellbottom pants that I found in a army, navy surplus store, which were hard to find at the time, and a blue cotton work shirt. Oh yeah, and beads. Wearing beads was like carrying a flag. It was the symbol of the counter culture.

Laura's mood lightened up even more after we got settled in our seats. I think the concert and the beauty of the evening considerably mellowed her mood. I know she was really excited when I got the tickets, and was touched when she realized that I went out of my way to get the best seats I could.

It was nearly dark when a man walked onto the stage to announce the opening act. No one was booked yet when I got the tickets, so I didn't know who it was going to be.

"Ladies and Gentlemen," his voice boomed over the sound system, "I am pleased to introduce a great American artist, Miss Joan Baez."

The crowd cheered. I was beside myself; I loved Joan Baez! I thought she had the voice and soul of an angel. I felt so pleased to be there; it seemed like a special night.

Joan walked out on stage carrying an acoustic guitar and stood in front of the microphone. Without saying a word, she just began singing. She was radiant. She possessed a balance of vulnerability, beauty, and feminine strength. Her voice was melodic, almost operatic, the words flowing light like the wind.

"Isn't she wonderful?" I asked, while smiling with pleasure.

Laura smiled back, and shyly said, "Thank you, for bringing me here."

I leaned over and placed a gentle kiss just behind her ear. The smell of her hair was intoxicating. "I'm glad you're having a good time," I whispered. She reached over and touched my hand.

Between songs, Joan would talk to the audience, making comments about the war or her music. Although I enjoyed the concert, Laura was really the one that captured my attention. I don't remember having ever seen her look quite so beautiful. I was seeing her as if for the first time: the shape of her lips, the color of her eyes, the way it felt when I touched her. She radiated sensuality. I couldn't imagine being more in love with her.

Joan began singing, "There But For Fortune." The crowd was spellbound. She didn't even need a guitar. Her voice carried the feeling of a thousand words. I felt high just listening to her. She sang a few Dylan songs too, which I thought was pretty brave since he was there. Songs like "A Hard Rain's A-Gonna Fall" and "It's All Over Now, Baby Blue."

There was a break between sets, so Laura and I got up and walked around. It was an unusually warm night, for that time of year, which was good for that guy in the loin cloth. Laura put her arms around me, and I wrapped mine around her and held her close. "What am I going to do?" she asked quietly.

I looked at her gently. "I love you." Her eyes started to well up with tears. She pulled away, wiping a few tears from her eyes. "What's wrong?" I asked, touching her arm. Like a typical guy, I wondered if she was having her period.

"I can't talk right now. I'll be right back," she said pulling away. All I could do was call after her. "But what's wrong?"

"I'll meet you back at the seats," she yelled, disappearing into the crowd.

I knew that chicks sometimes liked it when you chased after them, when they're upset, but I felt it was better not to. Besides, what was I gonna do? Burst into the ladies room? She wasn't normally like this. If she had been, I probably wouldn't have gone out with her for so long.

Slowly I started making my way back to our seats. There were people all around, talking, laughing, having a great time. Suddenly, despite all the noise and commotion of the crowd, there was a silence within me. I felt a strange peace, like nothing I had experienced before, yet at the same time it was familiar. I felt like I was in a separate reality. It was like I was there as a witness, simply observing.

Then, standing about twenty feet ahead of me, I saw a young man turned toward me. He looked different somehow. He had curly blond hair and his skin was almost luminous. I stopped in my tracks. It was like I was invisible, and he was the only one that could see me. There was something about him, something I had never seen before. Some quality that I can't explain. He looked at me deliberately, yet with a gentle kindness. Then he smiled. His smile filled me with joy. I could only laugh, I don't know why. I just laughed with joy. It was just a moment, but it felt like forever. I wanted to feel like that forever. I lowered my gaze for a second, and when I looked up again, he was gone. The sights and sounds of the crowd once again filled my consciousness. I looked all around, trying to figure out where he went. The whole thing was like stepping outside of reality for a moment. Normally, I would have said it was the pot, but I knew that it had worn off, and that experience was REAL.

I returned to our seats, and Laura was only a minute behind me. She leaned over kissed me. "I'm sorry. I don't know. I'm just going through something."

I touched her hand "Are you OK?"

"Sure, I'm OK." She assured me with a slight smile.

I wanted to talk to her more but Dylan was about to come on stage. I put my arm around her to comfort her and whispered, "I don't know what's up, but I'm sure it'll be OK." She didn't say anything. She just looked up at me with those beautiful green eyes.

I didn't think Dylan had a band, but when I looked up, I saw the stage set with drums and instruments.

"I've been thinking of going to Berkeley," she said, watching for my reaction.

I wasn't exactly sure what she meant, so I asked, "To see it?"

"They have a great psych. department. I don't know. I've been thinking of going to school there."

I thought that must be what she was jealous about with Sam and Silvia and their ability to get up and just go. I was about to respond when the MC got up on the stage. "Tonight's a very special night," he announced. I kissed Laura and said "We'll talk later."

The MC announced Dylan who came onto the stage wearing an worn pair of Levi's and a work shirt. He looked like he was one of us. For the next two hours he sang song like "Mr. Tambourine Man", "It Ain't Me Babe", "Blowin' In The Wind" and "Like A Rolling Stone". The audience was transfixed. People were smoking pot and passing it to their neighbors, but I was feeling really high just being there, so I would just pass them on. At the end, he sang my favorite song: "The Times They Are A Changin'."

The concert ended and the audience slowly cleared the theater. Laura and I stayed in our seats so we could talk. It was such a lovely night, and I had hoped that she was feeling better. But she sat with her head in hands, a wave of sadness washing over her.

"Why don't you tell me what's wrong?"

Laura looked up. "This isn't easy! Something happened a few weeks ago."

"What?" I had no idea what she was talking about.

"I was late!"

"Late for what?"

"You know! I, I thought that I was pregnant."

"You're pregnant? Oh, holy shit!"

"No I'm not! I only thought I was." She put her head in her hands again and sighed.

"So, everything's alright?" I asked with relief. I felt like I had just become a father and lost the baby in the space of one minute.

She realized my confusion. "It did something to me, it made me really think about what I wanted, what I want for my life." She stood up and leaned against the railing in front of us. "I've been really struggling with this."

I couldn't imagine what she was about to say. A million thoughts went through my mind. Maybe she wanted to get married. Maybe she was worried because we weren't careful enough. I used rubbers all the time. Well, most of the time. Sometimes, it's just not convenient. OK, no more excuses. "We'll be more careful in the future," I assured her.

"We can't keep seeing each other."

At first I didn't think that I heard her right. "What? Is this about Berkeley?"

"No. It's about us."

I felt like a knife had just been plunged into my heart. Suddenly I felt dizzy. This was not the night I planned for.

"It got me thinking about what I wanted to do with my life." She looked up and saw the tears starting to well in my eyes. "I'm sorry. I didn't want to hurt you."

I looked down because it hurt too much to look at her. I couldn't stop the tears from flowing. "We could work it out. A lot of people have long distance relationships."

"That's not it! My mind is made up. It's over, Trevor."

Another wave of pain went through my body. I was starting to feel sick to my stomach. I wanted to act tough then, but I couldn't stop crying. After a long silence, I realized that she was crying too.

"I love you too, but I just have to do this." Laura sat next to me and put her arm around me. I know she was trying to comfort me, but in my mind, it just showed me the love she was denying me.

I ripped off the silver cross I wore around my neck and handed it to her. My mother had given it to me. She said it belonged to my uncle and he wore it all through World War II. He believed it was the reason he survived

"What are you doing?" she asked, surprised. "I know this means a lot to you."

I didn't know what I was doing either: I was acting out of instinct, "That's why I want you to have it." I knew that it would be the last time I would see her, and the pain was almost unbearable.

The Hollywood Bowl was empty and quiet; they had turned out most of the lights. The drive home felt like it took hours.

Chapter 4

Decisions

That night I couldn't sleep. I lay awake rethinking the evening, trying to change the ending. I kept telling myself that this couldn't be real. She's going to come back; she'll call. She's just under too much stress from school. But I knew I was fooling myself. She never even called to see how I was doing.

I don't think I slept for the first week. I stayed up, working all the time just to keep busy, waiting for the phone to ring. Then, when it did ring and I recognized that it wasn't her, I just wanted to hang up so I wouldn't miss her call. The worst part of it was that my imagination was out of control. In my mind, I saw her out partying and dancing every night in that sexy red dress that I liked her in. I could see her at The Draft house, drinking a beer and laughing with some square guy in a polyester suit. The idea made my blood boil. How could she leave me for a jerk like that! I would sit there, stewing in my jealousy; then, I would remember that it was all in my head.

Could it be that she was alone and thinking about me too? What drove me nuts was that I would never know. I even tried getting high, but it just made me more paranoid.

The truth was that I felt a constant, deep ache in my heart. I thought of calling her again and again and again... each time talking myself out of it. The home that I loved so much was now the loneliest place on earth. I was either pacing the floor or calling friends, looking for a shoulder to cry on.

It didn't take long before I was wearing out all of my friendships. Nobody wanted to hear me go on and on about my ex-girlfriend. They were making excuses to get off the phone, saying, "Someone just came over" or "I've gotta be somewhere." Apparently they needed to be anywhere that was away from me. Even those who were compassionate in the beginning were starting to run out of patience. It was like that for weeks. No one came over anymore. I finally got the hint and stopped calling.

I was surprised one afternoon to get a call from Ellen. She was in tears. "I found Ernie with another chick." Her voice had that panicked sound like someone had just died.

I heard her words but wasn't sure if I understood. "Ernie did what?"

She took a few deep breaths to calm herself and continued. "I came home from work a little early today. I wasn't feeling good. When I drove up, his car was in the driveway."

She had my total attention, "Yeah, go on. What else happened?" She was still sniffling but sounded like she had regained some composure in her voice. "Are you okay?" I asked.

"Yeah... well, not really." Her shaky voice sounded like she was on the verge of bursting out in tears again at any moment.

I tried to comfort her, "I think I understand what you're going through. Just relax and be cool. I'm not going anywhere."

"I'm trying," she said as she drew another deep breath, then she went on, "I walked up to the front door and I heard the stereo blasting, so I let myself in." Her voice cracked and I could hear her start to sob a little again.

"Ellen? Are you sure that you want to go through all this now?"

She took a moment to calm down. "I went in the house; I guess he didn't hear me. Something seemed really strange. You know, I had this feeling in the pit of my stomach." Her voice broke again, and I was afraid that she would start crying.

"It's OK, I'm here for you," I said in a reassuring voice. It was the only thing I could think of to say. I mean, it was a real bummer that Laura left me, but the betrayal Ellen was going through was far worse.

She struggled on. "I went to the bedroom. The door was closed; I opened it just a little." It sounded like she was sobbing again.

"Are you alright? Is he still there? Where's Ernie?"

"He can go to hell!" Her voice sounded wounded and I knew that feeling. That feeling of being hurt and helpless to do anything about it.

"Do you want me to come over?"

"No, no. That's OK."

I wondered if he was there while she was giving me the blow-by-blow details. "Is Ernie there?"

"No, he's probably out balling his slut. I hope his dick falls off! I don't want to see his ugly face again!" There was a silence. I was feeling stunned.

"Trev?"

"Yeah?"

"Is it too late to take you up on your offer?"

"Which offer? Do you want me to come over?"

"No! It's too much like being at the scene of the crime. I don't want to be here when, or if, that son of a bitch comes back."

"Do you want to come over here? God knows, I haven't had company in a while. And you know how misery loves company."

She laughed. "Then we're perfect for each other. Besides, I really need to talk."

Ellen must have flown over. I'm sure she ran some red lights to get here in such a short time. She walked in with a six-pack in her arms. "I suppose Ernie won't miss these," she said with a sheepish grin. "And if he does, too damn bad!"

She seemed to dissolve in my arms when I hugged her. "Oh Trevor, I don't know what I'd do without you." She felt so vulnerable to me in that moment; it was a side of her I had never seen before. She had always been fun, a great friend to talk philosophy with. Now all of those outward trappings seem to wash away. Underneath she was so much more sensitive than she would have anyone believe.

I felt close to her. "Ernie must be crazy."

She peered up at me with a grateful look. Then her face changed, hiding her emotions. She hit me softly on the arm. "That he is, old friend. That he is." She walked over to the sofa and collapsed. "This has been a hell of a day."

I got us each a beer and sat down with her. "So you never finished telling me what happened?"

"Are you sure that you want to hear all of the sordid details?"

"What? Are you kidding? I'm the guy who has been crying on everybody's shoulder for the past two weeks. People are so sick of me that the operator won't even talk to me!"

Ellen laughed softly. "You're almost as pathetic as I am."

"Besides, it's comforting to know that I am not the only one who has gotten the shaft recently."

Ellen looked at me with a raised eyebrow looking just a little indignant at my inappropriate clowning.

"C'mon, spill! Pretend like I am Dear Abby."

"OK, Dear Abby, I found my asshole boyfriend in bed with another woman."

Mimicking an older woman I said, "Hmm, I think that Dear Abby would have recommended that you save sex until after marriage."

Missing the joke she continued, "I saw them in bed together, Trevor! That son of a bitch! I saw them. I grabbed what ever I could and threw it at him!"

"Wow! What did you throw?" I had an image of Ernie bleeding from a severe head wound in the emergency room.

"It was just a box of Kleenex. Although, I wish I'd had a brick," she chuckled.

"Who was the chick? Do you know her?"

Ellen took three big gulps of beer, then shook her head to get her hair out of her face. "First off, I've never seen her before. She looked like someone he found on the street, like she hadn't bathed in a long time. She smelled really gross. I don't know what garbage can he found her in."

This was a surprise because Ellen was always neat and clean. Even if she were wearing an old, torn pair of Levi's, they would be color coordinated with her blouse. "So did you talk to him? Did he have some kind of excuse?"

"Oh sure. He just happened to be walking through the bedroom while she happened to be lying there, in my bed, naked." She took a few more gulps of beer. "And then of course he just happened to trip and fall and his dick accidentally slipped inside her. Yeah, I'm sure that's how it happened."

"Wow, what a series of coincidences!" Ellen's angry eyes looked up at my comical expression and she laughed softly.

"Did you guys talk about what happened?" I asked again.

"Oh yeah, we talked! He said I didn't understand! Can you believe that asshole? I didn't understand! I didn't understand that he was sleeping around! You know, when they were handing out brains, I think he was in the back room smoking a joint." She guz-zled the rest of her beer and opened another one. "I guess they've been seeing each other for a while now." She laughed bitterly as she recalled his words. "And he said, that asshole, that they were 'in love.' It's like he was asking for my approval. It felt like I was a fuck-ing parent, and he was some kid in high school. It was surreal! Why the hell was I ever with that idiot? That shit head!"

She looked at me. "I've been thinking of leaving that asshole for a while. I just needed a reason. God I wish I would have! Do you know that he smokes pot every day now? To smoke a little at a party is OK, but all the time? Man, that really fucks you up!"

She shook her head. "Then, as if this wasn't enough, he asked me to wait there while he took her home. Her car was out of gas! That's when I called you."

"Well, are you ever going to talk to him?"

"No fuckin way!" She finished her second beer and opened another one. "So how are you doing? Did you ever hear from Laura?"

"No. Hey, maybe she's with Ernie!" We both broke up at that. It was especially funny because they couldn't stand each other's guts. It was a good cathartic laugh. Then it was my turn to unload. "I've been thinking about her in a different way. Maybe that helps me to cope with feeling so hurt."

Ellen sounded concerned. "Thinking about what?"

"She's more like her parents than I thought. Maybe more than she thinks. I thought she was a little more of a free spirit, you know? Now I'm convinced she's going to sell out, marry some guy with a Ph.D., squeeze out a few kids, and live in the suburbs until she dies. End of story!"

Ellen smiled and shook her head. I continued. "I want more. I just don't know what it is. I don't want to be like one of the cattle, off to slaughter."

"I know how you feel. I don't want to end up being part of American middle-class bullshit."

"I just feel like I've gotta do something!"

Ellen put her arms around me. She was soft and gentle. The warmth of her body felt comforting. "Why don't you crash here tonight?" I asked.

"Thank you," she said with relief. "I was going to ask you. I'm afraid he's going to come home, and I don't want to see or talk to him."

"Yeah, well, shit-head or no, I don't want you to kill him either, which might happen if you go back there!" We started to laugh and then the phone rang. Her body stiffened, and she looked scared.

"It's him! Don't answer it!"

I walked over to the phone as it continued to ring. Looking at Ellen, I shrugged helplessly. "I could let it go, but what if he comes over looking for you? I've gotta say something."

"Shit! Tell him you don't know where I am. Tell him anything. Just get rid of him!"

I picked up the phone. "Hello?"

"Hey man, it's Ernie!" His voice sounded like nothing had happened. "Have you seen my old lady, man?"

"Ellen? No man, I haven't seen her. Did something happen? Is she missing or something?"

"She just got pissed off and left the house. Now I don't know where she is!" He sounded confused.

Ellen came over and stood by me, trying to listen to the conversation. She could barely keep herself from yelling at Ernie. Just as she took a breath to speak, I placed my hand over her mouth. "Oh, really? What happened?"

"We had a little fight. She freaked out about something. She'll get over it!"

"It sounds bad, man."

"Well, if you see her, tell her I'm looking for her."

"Will do."

The phone line went dead. Ellen could barely contain herself. She was holding her fists clenched in front of her, like she was ready for a fight.

"OK slugger, he's gone."

"Can you believe that son of a bitch, that asshole, that fucker, that shit-head!"

"That coward, that mad man, that weenie, that thumb sucker..."

Ellen started laughing. "That bed wetter."

"Really? He wets the bed?"

Shortly after that, she calmed down and asked if I had anything she could change into. She thought that maybe Laura had left something.

I thought for a moment, taking a mental inventory of the closet. "Shit! I guess she was planning this for a while because she cleaned all of her stuff out of here. I've got bunch of T-shirts. I'm sure something will fit."

I went into the bedroom and started rummaging through my clothes looking for something she could wear. I had a box full of stuff I wasn't using. I didn't even know what was in it. Ellen came in and started looking at some of the stuff too.

"I don't think this is yours," she said, pulling out a cropped tie-top that belonged to Laura. She grabbed the tie-top and a pair of cut offs. "This will do fine. Is that OK?"

"Yeah, I didn't even know that stuff was there." I walked out of the bedroom so she could change. "Do you want him to move out?" I asked from the other room.

"No, I think I want to get out. It was Ernie's place to begin with. You know, I didn't even think she was that great looking. I think I'm better looking then her. I don't get it." She stepped out into the living room, putting her arms out and tilting her head back like she was modeling the latest fashion from Paris. I have to admit she filled out the top perfectly; it looked great on her. "Do you think I'm pretty?" she asked, not so much out of vanity but more like she wanted some reassurance.

"Yeah, I think Ernie's crazy. He really fucked up this time!"

"How about I make you dinner?" she asked, making herself at home.

I kind of liked this pampering. "Sure, knock yourself out!"

Ellen struck her modeling pose again and turned around. "You didn't say much. Don't you like it?"

"You're teasing me." I didn't tell her that I liked the teasing. Maybe I should have.

"Maybe a little."

I smiled. "I like it!"

She got to work in the kitchen, and I set a place to eat. I only had a small table in the kitchen, and it wasn't very comfortable, so I made up the coffee table with flowers and candles and a tie-dye tablecloth. We were going to dine picnic style in the living room.

It didn't take her long to whip up some spaghetti and garlic bread. It was far better than the TV Dinners I had been eating lately. I know it was an obvious question, but I had to ask. "Are going to leave him?"

She laughed out loud. "Well, what do you think?"

I shrugged my shoulders and put up my hands. "Hey, I was just checking!"

"I'm actually feeling OK about it now," she said calmly. "I almost feel relieved. I think I was looking for an excuse to leave him anyway, and now I don't have to feel guilty. I'm not even pissed off any more. She can have him. As a matter of a fact, I wish them well!" Then as an afterthought, she added, "They're gonna need it!"

I was a little confused. "I don't know how you can do that in such a short time."

"If I think about it, I could get really pissed off, but I don't feel like doing that." Her faced looked relaxed, as if everything was really OK. "Besides, I'm not really pissed off any more. I'm feeling more betrayed than angry."

She looked up and smiled. "Hey, I've got a groovy idea." I watched while she poured us each a glass of beer. She held hers up to make a toast.

"What are we toasting?" I asked.

"To a new beginning."

I put my glass down. "I think I'm still too hurt."

Ellen looked as though she was looking right through me. I couldn't hide anything from her. "You're just hurt?" she asked skeptically. "Are you sure you're not a little angry in there somewhere?"

I shrugged my shoulders. "Yeah, I guess I feel betrayed, and that kind of pisses me off." Ellen reached over and touched my hand. She was looking right at me, but I kept my head down. I think I was embarrassed, like I was a failure. "You need to let it go. Let go of her," she said resolutely. "Do you really think she's sitting around thinking about you?"

I wanted Laura to think about me, but I had to face the fact that she hadn't called. "I guess that does piss me off. I feel like I'm the victim of a hit and run. How could she cause me so much pain and then feel nothing? It's not fair! It makes me feel worthless, and I hate feeling like that. It's like she's taken away my self respect." All of the hurt that I kept deep inside was starting to rise to the surface.

Still holding my hand, Ellen tried to comfort me. "She was only thinking about herself."

"But I miss her so much!"

Ellen let go of my hand. "You'll probably never get over it!" she said, her voice more detached. I think it was her way of saying, 'get over it.'

The tears started to well up in my eyes. Ellen looked distraught at my reaction and came over and put her arms around me. "I'm sorry, I was just teasing you."

"I think that part of the pain is the indignity. After she broke up with me, I felt really worthless, ashamed of myself almost. Imagine having the woman you love tell you she wanted more for her life, and you knew what she was really saying was that you aren't good enough. Ouch! Now that I think about it, she's no better than Ernie. They're both selfish."

"That's why you have to let go of her. That kind of thing can really fuck with you. Besides, I think she made a big mistake."

"You're right, damn it!" I said, picking up my glass.

Ellen picked up her glass again. "To new beginnings and a new life." We clicked our glasses.

The phone rang again. I looked at her. "I think it's Ernie."

"Shit! If he knows I'm here, he'll come over!"

The phone rang shrilly again.

She looked up at me with that look like an Idea just popped into her head "Tell him Laura's here, then he'll leave you alone."

On the third ring of the phone, I picked it up, "Hello?"

I nodded to Ellen to let her know that it was him. She waved her hand as if gesturing me to go ahead. "Tell him. Tell him."

"Is that her?" ordered the voice from the other end. "Let me talk to her." He sounded desperate.

"Look man, I don't know where she is."

"Who's voice did I hear?" Ernie demanded.

"Laura's here, and I've gotta go. We need to talk. If I hear anything, I'll call you. OK?"

Ernie sounded almost like he was sobbing. "Sorry, man."

I wanted to get off the phone "OK, I've gotta go, and like I said, if I hear anything I'll call." I heard him hang up.

"I don't think he's going to call back." I said, sitting next to Ellen. "At least not tonight."

"Thank God! I'll deal with him tomorrow. You know I should have done this a long time ago."

"Catch them in bed?"

"Very funny!" Ellen said, punching my arm playfully. "No, I feel free, like a ton of weight has been lifted off my shoulders. I don't think I want to go back there again."

Then her voice dropped, "But I guess I have to. I hate shit like this! I'd rather not deal with it."

The thought had crossed my mind to let her stay with me until she found a place. I was a little afraid of how Ernie might react. I really hate having people pissed off at me, but I hate being alone even more. We had been friends for a long time, and I couldn't send her out with nowhere to stay. "Why don't you just stay here, until you find a place?"

"Really? Are you serious?"

"Yeah, it'll be fun!"

She practically lunged into my arms. "Thank you. I don't know what I'd do without you. Maybe tomorrow I'll go over while he's away. Then I can get my stuff, and I won't have to see him. I don't have much, just one chair and my clothes. It won't take very long. I'll just leave everything else."

"Ernie's gonna come over here eventually. Maybe you should just tell him."

"I can't think about that right now."

We stayed up and talked until it was quite late, managing to eventually talk about something other than our problems. When it came time for bed, I excused myself and went into the bedroom. I have to admit there was some sexual tension, particularly after all the beer, but I didn't want to complicate a good friendship. I didn't want to get involved, and I don't think she did either.

It was the first time in a while that I wasn't thinking about Laura. I had a friend who was in a similar situation, and I loved the company. The wind was blowing through my bedroom window. The breeze felt cleansing, like it was washing away all of my troubles. I got out my notes and carefully wrote down the events.

The following morning Ellen was already up when I awoke. It was nice to be greeted by her beautiful smile and a friendly "good morning."

"I found this in some of your stuff," she said, referring to an old t-shirt that she was wearing. "I hope you don't mind." Looking at me flirtatiously, she added, "I thought it would be better if I wore something. I usually don't wear anything to bed."

"I don't either." I would swear she was flirting with me, but I wasn't sure so I changed the subject. "Aren't you going to work today?"

"No, I called in sick about an hour ago. I don't think they believed me, but I don't give a shit. I want to quit that stupid job anyway. I hate the idea that I'm wasting my life filing bullshit papers for some warehouse. I spend half of my time wishing I were doing something else. But today I'm free."

"When are you going to pick up your stuff?"

She straightened some pillows. "I was wondering if, maybe, you could help me. Some of my things won't fit in my car. But it's OK, I'll understand if you don't want to," she added quickly.

"Is Ernie going to be there?"

"I don't know. He should be at work. I'll tell you what: if his car is there, we won't go in. How does that sound?"

"OK" I agreed, sighing. "Let's get it over with. But you know, you're gonna have to talk to him sometime."

"Yeah, some other time."

We left shortly after that. Just as we drove onto Topanga Road, I saw a hitchhiker. I always stopped to give a ride to other hippies. The guy looked harmless. He flashed me the peace sign and walked over to the van carrying a full backpack. He looked tall, and I could see that he was a bit older than me, maybe twenty-seven or twenty-eight. When he took off his hat, his curly brown hair fell down to his shoulders. He looked like he had been on the road for a while. Extending his hand to shake, he said, "Thanks for the ride, brother." He gave me one of those hip handshakes where your thumbs lock.

"Where are you headed?"

"I'm going to Haight-Ashbury, man. Is that where you're going?"

I thought it was a little strange that he asked that; we were hundreds of miles away from there. "No, we're just going down to Chattsworth, but I can drop you off at the freeway."

He sounded a little surprised. "Oh, sure, thanks." He paused for a moment and said, "I thought for sure you were going to San Francisco."

"What makes you say that?" Ellen asked.

"It's just a feeling I have. It's a strong feeling, or else I wouldn't have said anything. I do psychic readings."

Ellen turned sideways to face him. "Really? You're not just pulling our leg?"

The hitcher shrugged and smiled. "I do. I'm usually pretty accurate."

Ellen's eyes lit up. "What else do you see for Trevor?"

"I just get a feeling there's something there for him."

Ellen couldn't contain her curiosity. "What do you see for me?"

He looked intently into her eyes. "Let me take your hand."

She smiled at me with excitement and put her hand out to him. He closed his eyes. "I don't see you going north at this time, maybe later." Then he asked, "Are you two together?"

Ellen chuckled. "No, were just good friends."

"You're very close in a way," he said. "Your souls are close."

"What do you mean, our souls are close?"

"It's like you're soul mates. Have you always felt comfortable around each other? You know, like from the moment you first met."

"Yeah, we've always been like that." Ellen replied, with wonderment in her voice. "We always get along." I think she noticed my discomfort. I didn't want to get involved. I was afraid to get involved. It felt safe just being friends. Changing the subject, I asked, "What else do you see?"

He closed his eyes again. "Are you an artist?" he asked her.

"I want to paint and make clothes."

"You should," he replied, pulling his hand away gently. "Don't give up. I see you getting paid for your work. I see people handing you checks. You're life is about to change."

Ellen was in awe, but I was more skeptical. I mean he could be right, but how could you prove it? We were at the on ramp where I was to drop him off. Ellen asked one more question. "I know I'll probably never see you again, but what's your name?"

He smiled at her. "I'm Merlin. That's what everyone calls me."

Ellen reached over and gave him a quick hug. "Thank you," she said, in her kindest voice. "I think you have a special gift."

I reached out to shake his hand, he was sitting with one leg perched inside the van and the other already out. He looked back and grasped my hand, "Thanks brother," he said, grasping my hand again. "You should leave for San Francisco soon. I get a powerful vibration on this! Go soon! Don't worry about money or a place to crash. Things will work out."

"What do you mean?"

"I have a very clear vision. This doesn't happen very often, but when I touched your hand, it came to me. Besides, it's a beautiful place. You'll fit right in there!"

A chill ran down my spine. I could feel my hair stand on end. I couldn't put into words. It made me somehow uncomfortable.

As we drove away, I saw him giving us the peace sign. Ellen put her arm out the window and flashed him one back. She looked over at me and seemed aware of my distress. "Did Merlin say something that upset you?"

I felt queasy in the pit of my stomach. I tried to explain. "I don't know what it is." Ellen was facing me now, and it felt like she was probing. I felt like I needed to be alone to sort out what just happened, but clearly she couldn't wait.

"What are you feeling?" she asked.

"I'm feeling like I need something to eat. My stomach feels weird." Maybe that was it, I was just feeling sick.

Ellen looked out the window. "I think we've already passed everything. Maybe you can get something from the fridge when we get to my place. My old place, that is." She turned back to me. "Maybe you need to go, you know, to San Francisco."

"I'm thinking about going for maybe a week or so. I don't think I could afford to stay longer than that. But there's something else. I can't put my finger on it. It's a feeling; it kind of scares me. It's like, if I go, I feel like I could die there or something!"

"There's nothing to be afraid of," Ellen said tenderly. "Nothing's going to happen. It sounds exciting!"

"I can't just take off and go. I don't have that kind of money. And I don't want to lose my place. What if it doesn't work out up there?"

Ellen looked thoughtful. "Yeah, I see." We were silent for a moment, then suddenly Ellen's eyes lit up. She straightened and sat facing me. "I've got an idea!" She paused, attempting to draw me out.

"OK, what's your idea?" I asked slowly.

She sat back and calmly laid out her plan. "Well, as you know, I need a place to stay. You want to keep your place and can't afford to pay rent while your gone. So..." She stopped for a dramatic pause.

I knew where she was going, but I didn't want to spoil her dramatics. "So, what's you're big plan?"

She looked humored. "Do you really want to know?"

"Well, what is it?" I asked, playing along.

She turned away and looked out the window. "I don't think you really want to know."

It was cute the first time, but now I was starting to lose patience. "OK already! What the hell's this great plan?" I snapped.

"I'll stay at you're place and pay rent while you're gone. Well, what do you think?"

I looked down the road. "I'm thinking!"

"The last time you said that, nothing happened!"

I knew exactly what she was talking about, but I didn't want to say anything. I was feeling a lot of pressure. "OK, I'm going." I didn't even think about it. I'm usually not that spontaneous. It surprised even me. Just as I finished saying it, this feeling of peace came over me. It was like an affirmation. I really felt it would be OK.

Ellen looked at me with a sense awe. Her voice was soft. "Wow! Do you feel that?"

I could barely believe it. I felt completely at peace. "You can feel that too?"

"Oh, yeah!" She said it with such certainty that I had no doubt.

It's like a wave washed over me. I don't know how, but all of my doubts and fears vanished in that instant.

"You've gotta go! Don't worry about your place. I'll take care of it."

As we turned the last corner to her house, I saw Ellen's body tense up again. The momentary peace that she had felt just a minute ago drained out of her system. She was sitting forward in her seat looking for Ernie's van.

"Thank God, he's not here!" she said with obvious relief. "Let's do this really fast. I don't want to be here any longer than we have to be."

The house looked like an old farmhouse. It was small and it had some tall old trees in front. It sat on a large lot and had a fairly long

dirt driveway that billowed dust as we drove in. There were no sidewalks and the house was bordered by an old wooden fence that was
broken in several places. There were a lot of new houses in the
neighborhood. It looked like this one was here back when there
were still cowboys and cactus around. The house was a relic of the
past.

"You don't have to come in, if you don't want to," Ellen said getting out of the van. "I'm going to do this really fast."

We walked in the front door. "Everything look's OK," she said.
"He didn't throw away any of my stuff yet."

She took a duffel bag into the bedroom while I stayed in the living room. I looked around. There was a lava lamp and some magazines and rolling papers on the coffee table. I sat down and started
rummaging through the magazines. There was a copy of "Mad
Magazine" on the top and a "Fabulous Freak Brothers. Wow! Is this
yours?" I asked, thumbing through the Freak Brothers.

"Very funny!" Ellen said, coming to look over my shoulder.

I flipped through some pages and came to a slip of paper. There
was a name and a phone number on it.

"What does it say?" Ellen asked.

"Cari, 555-4321."

"I bet you that's her." She grabbed the paper. "Let's call the number."

"What?"

"Let's call the number. I want to know!" She grabbed the phone
and started dialing. She sat next to me and leaned over so I could
hear too. Ring... Ring... Ring...

"Nobody is there. Hang up!"

Then some girl's voice answered. "Hello?"

"Is Ernie there?"

"Ernie! I haven't seen him in months. Who is this?"

Ellen acted cool. "I'm sorry to be calling you. It's just that he's
been missing for a few days, and I don't know what's happened to
him."

"He's probably out fucking around. He could be anywhere. I feel
sorry for that guy's old lady. She doesn't know what the fuck is going
on."

Ellen was silent. She looked a little shocked.

"Hello? Hello? Hey, who is this?"

Ellen hung up the phone. She just sat there for a moment, then said, "Let's get the fuck out of here."

After we got home, I decided to take a hike. There was a trail that started at the end of the street that went into the mountains. I wanted to write while Ellen unpacked and settled in. I was feeling both excited and overwhelmed by the events of the day. With Ellen looking after my place, I felt free to go. Who knows? I might stay there or just turn around and come home.

I went to a place that looks out over Topanga Canyon. I could feel the moisture of the ocean, as a gentle breeze blew across my face. The wind felt fresh and renewing. I was in one of my favorite places. It was a place where I went to gather my thoughts. It's easier to see what I need to do when I'm there.

By the time I left the mountain, it was clear that I should leave in the morning. I felt like I needed to do it fast while the inspiration was still fresh. When I got home, I announced my decision to Ellen. She put her arms around me and said, "That's wonderful! We need to celebrate."

For some reason, I was feeling like this was a personal thing. I felt protective and didn't want to tell anyone else. Maybe I was afraid that they would think that I was crazy, because I was starting to feel that way myself. "I don't want to call anyone. Maybe the two of us could have a quiet celebration."

"That's exactly what I had in mind. Let's go somewhere for dinner and have a glass of fine wine."

"But, I'm not twenty one!" I laughed.

"OK, we'll get you a Shirley Temple," Ellen said, pinching my cheek.

The next few hours were busy. There was a lot to do. I had to go to the bank to withdraw my entire savings and pack whatever I thought I'd need for however long I might be gone.

Ellen hung a few of her things on the walls. She looked really pleased to be starting her new life. As evening drew near, Ellen took some time to get ready. She said she was going to wear a dress she had made and suggested I put on something special. The best I could do was a pair of black slacks, a long-sleeve white shirt, and a black tie. I looked more like a waiter than a customer, but it was all I had. I made a reservation at this cute little seafood place near Broad Beach. Then I sat on the couch and listened to the radio while I waited. They were playing this beautiful soft ballad, "Today," by the Jefferson Airplane. I shut my eyes for a moment and let myself drift with the music. "Today, I feel like pleasing you more than before... "

When I opened my eyes, Ellen was standing in front of me. Her hands were folded in front of her, and she looked a little shy. She was wearing a very short, blue chiffon dress with spaghetti straps. It had tiny pleats all the way around and it swung freely with every movement she made. She was wearing makeup like a fashion model, dark and rich for the evening. With her hair falling gracefully around her shoulders, she looked divine. She looked better than divine.

I just sat there with my mouth open, staring at her. Then she broke the spell. "Well, what do you think? And don't say, 'I'm thinking!'"

I felt high just looking at her. It was all I could do to say, "You look gorgeous, I mean, you really look gorgeous." I think she enjoyed my dumbfoundedness.

She stood there looking at me for a moment. I could feel my heart beating inside my chest. I think I was a second away from kissing her, when in a soft, deep voice, she asked, "Are you ready?"

We enjoyed a beautiful drive along the coast to the restaurant. It was a quiet, little place overlooking the Pacific. Ellen was beautiful. I felt privileged to be seen with her. I think the maitre d' fell in love with her at first sight. He walked up to her, completely ignoring me, and said, "I have a table by the window. Would you like that?"

"That sounds lovely," she answered with a calm elegance. Ellen looked like she belonged there. I bet he thought she was in the movies.

It was a charming place with a wood interior. The ocean side was wall-to-wall window to take advantage of the fantastic view of the ocean. Rope fishing nets with lots of starfish and abalone shells adorned the walls and ceiling. I couldn't help but notice as we passed Warren Beatty; at another table, I saw Michael Sarrazin.

After we were seated, the maitre d' lit a small candle that floated

like a lily pad in water. There were linen tablecloths and proper
cloth napkins. He asked us if we would like to start with a drink from
the bar. Ellen was two years older than I and casually ordered a glass
of white wine. I was afraid of the embarrassment of being carded, so
I put my head down like I was studying the wine list and said in my
most adult voice, "I'll have the same." He took my order without
question.

"There's Judy Carne," Ellen said in a whisper.

"Who's she?"

"Oh, that's right. You don't have a television set. She's on this
show called "Love On A Rooftop." It was really too bourgeois for
her, she explained, but she watched it 'sometimes.'

When our drinks were delivered, Ellen picked up her glass to
toast. "To wherever destiny takes us."

We clicked glasses. I felt closer to her than ever before. When she
looked into my eyes, I felt all the warmth and tenderness of her
soul. I wanted to stay in her company. How strange that I should feel
this now, just before leaving.

There had been several times in our friendship when I wondered
what it would be like if we…you know. I had a feeling she shared
these same thoughts. I think if someone were to ask me about Laura
at that moment, I would have asked, "Who? Who's Laura?" She was
quickly becoming just another memory.

We had a wonderful dinner, sharing a second glass of wine, and
talked about our plans for the future. Ellen wanted to find a way to
start selling her artwork and making custom clothes. "I've been
sewing since I was a kid," she explained. "I've got all of these ideas for
clothing designs that are just dying to get out. I've got some money
saved, and I want to take a chance. I'm feeling kind of dangerous."

"Well, what have you made?"

She put her arms up. "You're lookin at it."

"That's gorgeous! Or maybe it's the way you look, wearing it."

Ellen tilted her head down slightly, and then looked up at me. "I
believe you're flirting with me."

"Maybe just a little," I said, laughing.

She confessed that she fell into her relationship with Ernie for all
the wrong reasons. "I'm really happy it's over. I don't have to feel
bad or guilty. I can move on with a clear conscience."

"Are you going to call him?"

"I'm going to call him to say good-bye and wish him well with his life. I really don't want to talk to him at all, but I'll do it. I don't want to think about that tonight."

It was after sunset when we got back home. I had already given Ellen a key, so she went in first. I stayed out in the van and straightened up a few things for my sojourn. When I went in the house about ten minutes later, it had been transformed. Ellen had put candles all around. I counted seven on the coffee table alone. The curtain was open to the bedroom, and I could see candles back there too. She had covered the coffee table and couch with beautiful pieces of antique lace. The place was glittering. I was nearly speechless. It was such a beautiful sight.

Ellen looked timid and vulnerable and sexy, all at once. She leaned toward me and in her softest voice, she whispered, "I have a going-away present for you, and I'm not sure how you're going to react."

I put my arms around her and pulled her close, our bodies pressing against each other. I looked into her eyes just long enough to show her the passion that was burning inside me. Then I kissed her. It felt like sweet poetry. We kept sharing deep kisses, stopping only for moments to gaze at each other.

I held her face like it was the most precious thing on Earth. Looking into her eyes with concern, I said, "But I'm leaving tomorrow."

She smiled softly. "It's OK. I want to be with you tonight." She kissed me tenderly on the lips. I closed my eyes and felt like I was floating. Her soft, warm embrace permeated the essence of my being.

She took my hand and led me into the bedroom. Slowly, she unbuttoned my shirt. Her slinky dress only had one button in the back; I reached behind her and carefully undid it. We were both smiling, unable to conceal the pleasure we were experiencing. I slid one of the thin spaghetti straps off her shoulder. I kissed her neck and shoulder as it slid down, revealing one of her breasts. Her head moved back slightly in a gesture of complete surrender to the pleasure. I slipped off the other strap, and the dress slid helplessly to the floor. The exquisite shape of her naked body was highlighted by the

soft glow of the candlelight. She removed my shirt and slacks, and
we lay down, locked in a warm embrace. I felt safe and secure in her
arms. We were like two strings on a violin vibrating in harmony. I felt
overwhelmed with a deep love that transcended any previous love I
had known. I just let myself be immersed in the moment. Our bodies tingled with each tenderness we lavished upon each other.

The first thing I saw in the morning was light streaming through
my bedroom window. I felt a deep sense of contentment, as I lay in
bed watching her sleep. She looked peaceful. Her silky dark brown
hair spread across her bare back. She stirred, and her eyes opened
sleepily to see me lying beside her. I touched her shoulder, stroking
her hair, my hand moving along her back. She closed her eyes and
smiled. She was a picture of contentment. "Mmmm..." was the only
sound she made. I leaned over her to kiss her back and shoulder.
"You're spoiling me. If you keep this up, I won't let you go."

"I'm not sure if I still want to."

She looked at me seriously. "I think you have to! We'll still be
friends when you get back."

I felt a frustration at not being able to articulate how I felt. "I
want you to know that last night was... very special." I wanted to say
more but I couldn't find the right words.

"I felt free being with you. I didn't know that was possible. Men
have always tried to own me. But with you, I feel free. That's a great
feeling. I don't feel like you want to run my life."

"Maybe I shouldn't."

"Wait! Let me finish my thought. Yesterday when we gave that
guy a ride, I felt something when I saw him shake your hand.
Remember, he said you should go soon."

I knew exactly what she was talking about, but I didn't say anything. I was amazed that she had experienced the same thing I did,
only vicariously.

"I felt like he was telling the truth," she continued. "I felt a tingling all over me. Did you feel anything?"

"Yeah, I felt the same. I don't know what this is all about. I mean,
it's really not that far away."

"I don't know why, but this is for you alone. Who knows? Maybe
you'll run into Sam and Silvia."

"Silver," I corrected her.

She laughed. "You can give me a whistle, let me know how you're doing. You know how. Just put you're lips together." She tried to whistle, but it came out flat. "Well, you know the rest."

After a bit, I gathered a few last things and walked out to the van. Ellen walked out with me. I looked back at my house longingly. She kissed me and said, "Maybe you'll find what you are looking for."

I drove away, wondering if I'd ever return. I could feel the wheels grinding on the pavement below, my thoughts of the night before now a sweet memory.

Chapter 5

Big Sur

For the past month, I had been hearing ads on the radio for the Monterey Pop festival. I thought of going, but it was too far away and I always had something more important to do. I was always too busy. Now suddenly I wasn't! The festival was going to run for three days and would feature some new artists like Jimi Hendrix, Big Brother and the Holding Company and The Jefferson Airplane. I hadn't really considered it, but now that my whole world had turned upside-down, anything was possible.

By the time I hit the road, the festival was only days away. I had heard that it was sold out so I didn't bother to purchase a ticket. Following the spirit of my journey, I just went on faith, hoping that it would work out.

Highway 1 is a picturesque drive that winds along the coastline all the way to Monterey. Even though I'd lived in California my entire life, I'd never traveled this far north. So I embarked with a sense of excitement. It was hard to believe that only yesterday, these were all just places on a map to me and now, I was going to experience them.

My first stop was at a place in Santa Barbara that I later learned was known to hitchhikers as "the lights." It's a long grassy area along the side of the highway where there's a series of traffic lights. It's a perfect place for hitchers to catch a ride up or down the coast. Hitchhikers can lie on the grass, take a short walk to get something to eat, or walk down to the beach.

I saw a couple holding a brown cardboard sign with "Monterey" scribbled across it, in black magic marker pen. From the van, I could see them smiling and laughing. They looked safe; they also looked like they were having a great time talking and laughing. So, I pulled over to give them a ride.

An unshaven but friendly looking guy walked up to the passenger side of the van. I slid open the window as he leaned down to look at me. I think he was checking me out to see if it was safe to get in.

Tipping the brim of his straw hat to shade his eyes, he asked, "How far are you going?",

"All the way to Monterey."

He sounded excited, "Psychedelic." He looked back at his girl-friend and waved to her to come over. She grabbed their shabby duffel bags and ran toward the van.

To avoid me looking like a chauffeur, he took the passenger seat beside me while his partner got in the back of the van.

"Hey, thanks man!"

I responded, "No problem! My name is Trevor. What's yours?"

"Mark," he cheerfully answered.

The girl leaned forward, putting her head between Mark and myself and said, "My name is Terra." Her voice almost sounded babyish, yet it seemed to fit her small frame. She seemed interested in talking; yet her eyes showed that her time on the road had taken a toll on her. She looked exhausted.

"How long were you out there?" I asked.

Mark answered while Terra lay back against some pillows I had in the back. We were only out there for about an hour, which isn't bad. Since we got to California, getting rides has gotten a lot easier."

"Where are you both from?" I asked.

Mark answered again, "We're from New York. Have you ever heard of a place called Mount Kisco?"

"Is that where you're both from?" I answered, "You're a long way from home."

"Yeah", Mark laughed good naturedly.

"Where is Mount Kisco? Is that in upstate New York?"

"No man, it's only about an hour away from New York City. It's a nice place, but there's nothing to do there. When I get back, I'm moving down to the City."

"New York City? I've never been there."

Mark explained "It's cool. There are a lot of hippies in this part of the city they call 'The Village.' When I get back I'm moving there, so I can spend more time studying for school. I've gotta flying back after the festival."

"The festival! Are you going?"

"That's why we're here."

I looked in the rearview mirror and saw Terra sleeping, curled up in a ball. Mark explained to me how it was usually hard to sleep while you're on the road. He said that he was glad to see Terra crashed in the back. He explained that they had been gone for almost two weeks and she really needed the rest. "When you're hitching, you have to be looking over your shoulder all the time. Especially a chick," he added.

I assured him, "It's a long drive up the coast, and she can sleep all day if she wants." It turned my stomach to think that somebody would have ill intent toward these travelers.

"So, what do you do in New York?

"He took a troubled breath and answered, "I'm going to school at New York University. I'm majoring in sociology, and it's kicking my ass. I have to maintain a high GPA to keep my student deferment from the draft. I've been right on the edge for the past year, and it's a little scary, man!" Then he looked at me and added, "The only other way out, for me, is to move to Canada."

"I hear you, brother. If you went to Canada, what would you do?" I asked.

Mark looked down and shook his head. "It's fucked, man. I'd have to renounce my American citizenship. I don't want to do that. But I don't want to die for some weapons manufacturers, or some shit like that!" He looked at me again, curious. "Hey, aren't you over eighteen? How are you staying out of it?"

I didn't tell my story too often because sometimes people would react strangely. I could almost sense a hidden anger in they're reactions. They seemed to fall into one of two groups. The first group is pissed off because they see me as being some kind of coward that doesn't want to fight. The other group is jealous because they want a way out, and can't think of one. I was careful about telling people; I didn't want to rub my good fortune the wrong way. Mark seemed pretty open so I decided to and tell him my story.

"About three years ago I spent a few days in the hospital. My parents checked me in for testing. My folks are both very liberal.

They're both opposed to the war, and they didn't want to see me have to go through it. So they made an appointment and sent me to the hospital, where they checked everything imaginable. They had me running treadmills, with all kinds of wires attached to me. They must have taken a hundred separate blood samples. You name it, and they did it. Eventually I was diagnosed with a mild heart condition. My doctor is this Austrian guy who lived through World War II and he told me that he doesn't want to see anyone ever go to war again. I also saw this draft counselor who showed me where to mail my medical papers. The draft board eventually sent me a draft card with a 4F, a medical deferment."

Mark looked slightly envious, "Wow! That's fuckin great! Maybe I could find a doctor like that!"

We drove past Morro Bay where the Highway travels right along the shore, along some of the most beautiful scenery in the world. The air was thick with moisture, and the fog hovered like clouds off the cliffs. Driving with my window open, I felt the moisture embracing my face like tiny raindrops.

Terra was wide-awake by then and climbed over to the front of the van, sitting between the two of us. "I was feeling lonely back there," she said.

The front seat was a long bench and had barely room for all three of us.

"Well, it looks like you're wide awake now," Mark said, inspecting her eyes.

Terra took a deep breath and answered "Yeah, I feel great." She looked my way. "I haven't had a chance to really sleep since we left New York. You know, there's always some asshole checkin' me out. We got a lot of rides from truckers. This one guy talked for nine hours about some chick that gave him a blow job ten years ago."

"One year ago," Mark corrected.

Terra barely concealed the annoyance in her voice "Yeah well, I thought he was gonna write a fuckin' book about it."

Mark smiled and said sarcastically, "He probably had to pay for it." Mark had his wallet out, and he was searching through it, looking for something.

Terra not paying any attention to what Mark was doing asked, "Hey, Trevor, are you driving home after the concert?"

"No, I'm going up to Haight-Ashbury."

Terra looked impressed, she raised her voice a little "That's what I'm doing!"

"You're not going back with Mark?" I asked, surprised.

"Oh," Terra giggled and looked over at Mark,"No, this is something I've gotta do. I came along because I know I have to go to San Francisco. Mark and I've talked about it."

Mark just grunted while being distracted with something else.

Terra continued "We'll still be friends."

Feeling like I'd become friends with Mark, I looked over at him and asked. "Why don't you come along man?"

"I can't." His voice had a tone of resignation. "I can't. I gotta get a job to earn money for school. You know, I gotta fight the fuckin' draft."

Unfolding a sheet of paper from his wallet, he said, "Oh good, I found it!" ,his voice was upbeat again as he unfolded a sheet of paper he had in his wallet, "I just want to make sure that it's still there."

I looked over and saw the paper. It had about a dozen blue dots on it. Terra looked at it like it was something really cool. At the risk of sounding naive, I asked, "What is it?"

"It's blotter, man," Mark said with reverence in his voice."It's blotter." I must have had a blank look on my face, so he explained, "It's acid."

I'd never seen anything like it. "Do you mean those dots of ink? I thought it came in sugar cubes."

"This is new. I bought it from this guy in The Village. He makes it in his apartment."

I was feeling a bit nervous. Just what I needed, two people tripping out on acid in my van. To top it off, we would probably get pulled over too! Cops were not hip about my long hair. "Uh, guys, you're not going to do that right now, are you?"

"No man, I've been saving it for this weekend," Mark said, placing it carefully back into his wallet.

I felt a huge sense of relief. I knew everyone was doing it, but I was afraid. I had heard some weird stories of people seeing things that weren't there. There were also those folk legends of someone jumping out a window. But even some of the real stories made me uneasy. One guy I had met told me about how he wandered around lost in the Valley. He was on foot and he didn't know where he was. He told me he couldn't even remember his name.

Mark seemed pleased with himself after having found it, he snuggled up against the window and went to sleep. It was around sunset when we finally reached Big Sur. The drive was beautiful, but I felt a little nauseous from all the hours of twists and turns.

Big Sur was amazing. There were hippies everywhere. They were all going to Monterey for the festival.

I saw a campground and pulled in. Just as I did, a camper sped away; the people seemed upset. The woman at the booth told me I was in luck: there was only one camping space left. She said a family from Covina decided not to stay. We parked in the empty space, and I immediately got out and walked around. I was aching from sitting so long. It was a pretty drive, but nine hours is enough for anyone to bare, in a bumpy and noisy van.

As I looked around, I was amazed at the scene. The campground looked like a big love-in. I saw people dancing, singing, talking, and laughing. It's like it was one big family. The little log boundaries that were set up didn't seem relevant. People were sharing everything they had, and you could sleep anywhere you wanted to. It would have been bad etiquette to say no to your brother or sister. And that's what it felt like.

The people in the space next to us invited us to join them. They were sitting around a big campfire and it looked like they were cooking hot dogs with wire coat hangers to spear the dogs.

"Are you hungry?" a man with long white hair called out to us.

"Sure!" Mark yelled back.

"Come on over. We've got more than we need."

There must have been eight or ten people sitting around the fire. One by one, everyone introduced themselves but I forgot their names just as soon as I heard them. The guy who invited us over called himself Paco. I couldn't imagine where he got his name, because Paco was clearly an older English gentleman but he dressed like a young hippie and kept his long white hair neatly tied back with a leather cord. He was wearing a pair of khaki trousers that looked like they were from the English army and a rainbow colored vest.

Sounding a bit like George Sanders he asked, "Are you going to Monterey then?"

"Yeah!" Mark answered excitedly.

"I just came up from LA this morning," I added.

Paco was roasting a hot dog. "I usually don't eat this kind of food. You see, I don't know what it's made of. I believe in only putting natural things in my body."

"What's not natural about a hot dog?" Terra asked.

Paco's face lit up. He was clearly pleased to have someone's interest. "What I am attempting to explain is that I usually don't care to eat foods that have a questionable origin. For example, I have been appraised that good old American hot dogs are made of various sections of an animal, in this case the pig. These are parts that most individuals wouldn't normally consume if they knew what they were eating."

Terra shrugged her shoulders. "Like what?" She examined her hotdog to see if it was done cooking.

"Oh, like the lips, nose, ears and.. well, you get the idea."

"Ewww." Terra looked repulsed, almost to the point of foregoing the food for that day. She must have decided that was a bad idea because she took a bite of her hotdog anyway. "So, what do you eat?"

Paco leaned forward and explained "I make every attempt to eat fresh fruits, fresh vegetables, and grains. It is critical that people learn what's good for them." He paused for a moment as though he was trying to construct his next thought. "I'm looking to start a healing school, and teach these principals."

"What do you mean? For doctors?" Terra asked.

"No, not exactly. I'm talking about a training center for a different type of doctor. There are other modalities for healing the body. I want to introduce healing methods from around the world. For example, in England many people use a type of medicine called Homeopathy."

I was getting interested in their conversation, so I plopped down next to Terra. Someone passed me a joint, and I took a hit. I wasn't sure if I heard him correctly. "What kind of medicine?"

Paco looked at me, but continued his train of thought. "And they use something in the Orient called Acupuncture. I was on holiday in Japan, about fifteen years ago, and managed to injure my back. I must have pulled a muscle. I was in a tremendous amount of pain. Some chap that I was traveling with suggested that I go to a local traditional doctor. Well, to my utter amazement, this doctor placed thin needles in my back and ankles. I began to feel better that afternoon, and by the next day, the pain was gone! I don't know how it worked. It was truly a miracle!"

Terra looked confused. "Needles! He put in needles? Do you mean he gave you shots? Didn't that hurt?"

"No, it didn't hurt at all these were tiny needles," Paco explained. "He inserted them into my back with very little pain. The only sensation I felt was a light tingling. He kept them in my back for about twenty minutes. I can't imagine how it worked, but it did.

"What were these needles made out of? Did they have some kind of medicine on them?" Terra asked, still trying to understand.

"No, they were just needles. It's where you put the needles that matters. The doctor told me that there are channels in the body where energy travels, and he can increase or decrease the flow of energy by using needles. This energy is what heals you." Paco went on. "I want to bring these ideas to America. All I need is about twenty acres somewhere in the woods." He gestured with his hand, waving it through the air like he was showing us his school.

He showed us drawings, outlining the buildings he wanted. He had even planned an amphitheater for outdoor classes.

It was all interesting, but I had been sitting in the van all day and I was feeling like I needed to move. I excused myself and walked around the camp ground. The air was filled with the scent of campfire smoke, pot, and incense. Everywhere I went, I heard live music echoing through the forest. I walked by one campsite where a large teepee was set up. There was a group in front of it playing guitars, flutes, and bongos. They didn't sound that great, but they didn't seem to notice. They were clearly having a great time.

Then I walked by an old school bus painted in bright psychedelic colors. It had the top part of an old VW van welded to its roof. There was a small group sitting outside talking. I paused for a moment to look at the bus, and this gal signaled me with her arm. "Come on over and join us." They looked at least ten years older than me, but I was fascinated by the bus so I wandered over to find out more.

"Have a seat. I saw you standing there, and you looked interested, so I thought I'd invite you over. My name is Elisa."

I took a seat on one of the benches they had set up in a circle and joined in the conversation.

"Whose bus is this?" I asked.

Elisa pointed to a graying haired man sitting on the other side of the circle who greeted me, "Hi, my name's Ed.

He saw me stealing looks at the bus, and smiled at my curiosity, "Why don't you go on in and take a look," he insisted. "Just go on in."

I was surprised to see that it didn't look anything like a school bus. Cabinets were built into both sides of the metal walls. It had a stove, a sink, and even a tiny bathroom. The back of the bus had a couch that folded out to a double bed. It was pretty impressive. When I went back out, I thanked Ed for the self-guided tour. "Is this where you live?"

Elisa answered, "It's Ed's, but for the next few weeks we're all living in it."

I would guess her to be around thirty-five years old; she seemed a generation apart from me. She was pretty, but she wore her hair in a weird-looking flip, and with all of that hair spray and make-up, she looked like some chick from an old James Bond film. I was afraid she'd get too close to the fire and her head would turn into a human torch. I know she was trying to be hip, but she looked seriously out of place. I'd see women down in LA that looked like her. The aging beauty queen about ten years past her prime.

Ed explained, "We were talking about dreams we've had when you joined us. Elisa was just about to tell us about a dream she had last night." He turned his attention to Elisa. "Go ahead and tell us. What happened?"

Everyone was quiet, waiting for her to speak. "Well..." she looked down, it was obvious she was trying to remember,"I slept outside last night, over there," she said, pointing to the ground. "And in my dream, I was there in my sleeping bag. I thought I had awakened. I stood up and started to walk around. Then I looked back and saw my body lying there still asleep. I saw people everywhere, but they were all like ghosts." She looked around at all of us sitting there. "They were all see-through."

"Don't you mean translucent?" a man asked in a snobbish voice.

Thinking I was wrong about her, I urged her to continue. "Go on" I said, "what else happened."

She concentrated again. "I don't think they knew I was there. Some of them were dressed in old-fashioned clothes, like from a hundred years ago, and there were a lot of Indians among them."

Ed asked, "American Indians?"

"Yes, I think they must have lived here. They were all wandering about. Many of them were talking but I don't know what they were saying. It was just all chatter to me. Nothing distinguishable."

"What else happened?" I asked, fascinated.

Elisa focused her attention on me and answered, "Well, then I looked up and I saw that there were angels everywhere, there must have been a thousand of them. As soon as I saw the angels, I was among them. I don't know how this happened, but in that moment, it all seemed perfectly natural. One of the Angels flew over and touched me. I felt a sensation run from the crown of my head down through my whole body. It felt almost sensual. It was wonderful!"

"What did they look like?" I asked.

"They look the way you probably think they would. They have wings, and they're luminous. They don't have halos like in the paintings, but they have a glow of light that surrounds them. They're really very beautiful."

"Did they use their wings to fly?"

She thought for a moment "It's more like they move by thought. She looked like she was struggling to find the right words "... I believe they communicate through thought too."

I didn't disbelieve her, but I tend to be very rational. "How do you know it wasn't just a dream?"

Elisa sat back. "It was as real as this conversation. I can't give you any proof, but I know in my heart that it was real."

"I believe you," I assured her. "I don't think you'd make up something like this. So how did it end?"

Her voice suddenly sounded more solid as if she had come back into her body, She sounded more present. Her resonance even changed. "I just woke up. I opened my eyes, and I was back in my body, back in my sleeping bag. I'll never forget how beautiful they were. I think they're always around, but we just can't see them."

We talked a while longer and I thought she was being really friendly, but I was feeling a bit out of place. I got the impression that she was being a little too friendly and I wasn't interested. She was sitting a little too close, and she kept touching me while she was talking. After a while it was making me feel uncomfortable.

I went back to my van quite late and didn't see a trace of Mark or Terra. So I made some notes in my journal and turned in.

Chapter 6

Monterey

There was only silence when I awoke to the crisp morning air. Looking outside my van window, I saw that the world was still and silent. There were only a few birds hopping around, picking up some leftover crumbs, along with the squirrels who were also out scavenging for leftovers.

Mark and Terra were sound asleep outside the van. I quietly stepped out to the same paved road that I had walked the night before and found myself in the midst of huge redwood trees. Stopping to look straight up, I nearly lost my balance. The trees were so tall that I could not see their tops.

I walked by the teepee I had seen the night before. There was a woman sitting outside doing yoga exercises. I had only heard of yoga recently at a lecture in Santa Monica. It was beautiful to watch. She moved gracefully in slow fluid movements from one position to the next. Not wanting to disturb her concentration, I tried walking very carefully past her to not to make a sound.

The lingering scent of charred wood mixed with the fresh morning air filled my senses. It felt wonderful to be there. I normally didn't wake up at this hour, but I think it's my favorite time of day. There's a peaceful stillness when the world is still asleep.

Eventually I made my way back to the van to find Mark sitting up in his sleeping bag. His thick black hair was matted and dirty. He looked like he badly needed a shower. He greeted me with a friendly smile. "Hey man, I got you tickets for all three days."

I was thrilled, "Wow! Really? How'd you do that?"

"I traded some of those blue dots."

I was overjoyed "Oh man, thanks! That's so groovy! What do I owe you?"

He pulled the tickets from the backpack next to him and offered them to me. "You better take it now just in case we don't see each other after we get there."

What a relief! Until then, I wasn't sure if I was going to be able to get in to the concert, especially when I saw all the people that were turning out for it. "I can't tell you how happy I am," I said.

"That's what it all about! You don't owe me anything."

After a short while, Terra and Mark were up and on their feet. There was a faucet sticking out of the ground, which we used to wash up. I put my head under it and washed my hair. The water was freezing cold and it felt like a thousand little needles when it hit my body, but I couldn't stand feeling dirty any longer. We took turns washing and by the time we were through, we were wide awake and ready to go. Everybody was excited about getting up to Monterey.

I was immediately charmed by the beauty of the town. We drove along the shore by Cannery Row before going on to the festival. Even the poetry of a Steinbeck novel couldn't capture the atmosphere of Monterey. The costal pines twisted their way to maturity like large bonsai trees with faint clouds of mist clinging to them before they evaporated into the morning sun. The town was lined with cute wooden cottages, each different in their design. It was still early so we stopped to take in a few of the sights before the festival.

Shortly after we arriving at the fairgrounds, we were separated in the crowded love-in atmosphere. I enjoyed seeing the different types of people and different attire. People were dressed in everything from old Levi's to vibrant psychedelic colors. It seemed that people from all walks of life were there. I saw the rich Hollywood types, flower children, and folks that looked like they came out of the suburbs. I don't know where I fit in, but it didn't really matter. There was a place for everybody. We were gathered here for a unique purpose, like a gathering of the tribe. There was a feeling in the air that things were changing and we were all a part of something much greater than ourselves. I was being an optimist, but I really thought that for perhaps the first time in history, the world would wake up and see that we don't have to hate and we don't have to fight anymore. It felt like this was the dawning of a new age on Earth.

The festival began on the evening of June 16. John Phillips from the Mamas and the Papas walked out on stage to deliver the opening announcements and the first Tribal-Love-Pop festival began. At least that's what I heard some people call it.

The Association, Lou Rawls, Johnny Rivers, Eric Burdon & The Animals, and Simon & Garfunkel all performed that first evening. Everything went beautifully. The official theme of the weekend was love and flowers, and the feeling of the crowd reflected it. People were sharing everything they had. I even saw someone give his jacket to a stranger who was feeling a little too cold in the chilly evening.

It was common for someone to light a joint and pass it to the person next to them, who would pass it to another person and so on. All you had to do was sit there and sooner or later, a joint or a bottle of wine would come your way. It might be from someone behind you or someone next to you. You just took some and passed it down; that was the etiquette. The drugs were flowing freely and everybody was doing it. Someone sitting near me was lighting sticks of incense, and the scent would travel past me. It was an intoxicating odor, one that I always associate with that night.

The second day began earlier. The intensity was high. By evening, it was palpable. It really felt like the energy was turned up. Canned Heat started the afternoon with some Southern California blues. The evening brought acts like The Byrds, Laura Nyro, Jefferson Airplane, Big Brother & The Holding Company, and Otis Redding.

I saw an empty seat up front near the stage, so I went over and sat in it like I belonged there. No one said anything. I relaxed and watched The Jefferson Airplane perform. I'd just seen them a few weeks earlier at a love-in in Elysian Park down in Los Angeles. The Airplane and The Grateful Dead had played for free that day. A woman sitting next to me passed me a bottle of wine. I took a few gulps and passed it on. It was very sweet, more like grape juice than wine.

After a while, another group took the stage. They were Big Brother & The Holding Company with lead singer Janis Joplin. I'd only heard them a few times on the radio, but I liked what I heard. The weather was perfect. White puffy clouds floated across the sky, and stars were visible where there were no clouds. Everything was starting to take on a shine. It all looked perfect, or maybe I was feeling so good that everything I saw seemed perfect. I don't know what it was; I was just in love with the evening.

I turned my attention back to the stage. I felt deeply connected to Janis Joplin. It felt like she was psychically linked to every one within the range of her voice. I saw waves of translucent energy flow from her and ripple over the audience. She appeared more like a spirit than a person. Her actions seemed to emanate from the very core of her soul, expressed through her body without any hesitation. It was like she didn't have the same separation from her spirit that most of us experience. There was an honesty, a naked vulnerability about her. Her voice was a pure reflection of her soul with no ego in the way. When she finished the song 'Ball and Chain,' the audience was cheering. It was an amazing moment in time. One I'll never forget.

When the noise quieted down, the woman sitting next to me leaned over and said, "How are you doing? Are you there yet?" She was on the same wavelength as me. When she looked at me, I could see a deep honesty in her soft green eyes. She was older than me by probably ten years, but her spirit was ageless.

I felt in love with everything throughout all of creation. It's like I could sense the presence of God living in all things and see the beauty of the divine. She put her hand on my shoulder. It seemed like an eternity had passed since she had asked the question. She moved closer to my ear and in a deliberate slow pattern asked, "How are you feeling?"

I started to speak, but I wasn't sure if I could remember how to talk. It was like I had no language. Somehow I managed to say, "Beautiful! Everything's love! It's all alive!"

"I understand," she said, her voice warm and nurturing. "Go with it, wherever it takes you."

A mosquito landed on my arm. My instinct had always been to swat them. This time was different. I noticed there was something more alive about it. I understood that it had a soul too. I looked at the mosquito and felt a deep love for it. I felt that we were mentally communicating. She felt the love and returned love. In that moment, there was an agreement that I wouldn't kill mosquitoes anymore, and they wouldn't sting me. The mosquito flew away, and I didn't see any more of them.

I didn't have time to think about what I was experiencing. It was all unfolding naturally. I never stopped to think, "I can't talk to a mosquito!" It was perfectly normal and natural at that moment. I realized that I was experiencing life at a higher level of consciousness. I could see and understand the subtleties of cause and effect. I saw how our interactions carry energy, and how on a deeper level everything is energy. Our personalities are nothing more than our egos seeking self-recognition.

Even though my legs felt like rubber, I decided to get up and walk around. Another band was on stage, and I could hear the rhythm of the sound behind me as I wandered. There were people everywhere. I'd walk past them, looking into their eyes as I drifted along, almost gliding. I could see peoples' egos at work. There is a wall of personality we put up that prevents us, all of us from seeing our real selves, that deeper core of who we really are. You know, the party personality, the recluse, the freak, the saint. "I'm an artist" or "I'm Italian" or "I'm a hippie," etc. There are thousands of masks to choose from, but underneath it we're all the same.

Eventually, I found a grassy area and lay down. I looked up at the clouds and watched them glide past. I could feel and hear the waves of music as I lay there under the glow of the California summer night sky. I looked at all of the blades of grass, and I could see that each one had a life force. They would vibrate in a subtle harmony every time the wind blew.

It didn't dawn on me that I had taken LSD until sometime late that evening. It must have been in the wine. I allowed myself to enjoy the experience I was high most of the night and stayed up taking notes. I desperately wanted to describe the experience while the memory was still fresh.

The last day of the festival opened with a moving raga by Ravi Shankar. It was just what I needed. The music had a healing quality to it. My body was aching all over. It felt like even my bones and teeth were aching deep inside. After that, the few times a bottle of wine came my way, I just passed it on.

I thoroughly enjoyed the rest of the show. I believe there was magic in the air.

Chapter 7

The Fortune Teller

The grassy parking lot quickly ground into dirt as thousands of wheels rolled over it, stirring clouds of dust into the air as they passed. I waited until the lot had nearly emptied. It crossed my mind that they might have gotten another ride and just as I was about to join the long line of traffic, I saw them off in the distance. Terra was waving her arms trying to get my attention but I could barely hear her calling. They casually sauntered across the now vacant lot while Terra was trying to get a brush through her long matted hair. They both looked like they had just awakened.

I helped Mark remove his heavy backpack while he sat down on the ledge of the open double side doors. He was huffing like an old man and lit a cigarette as soon as he sat down.

"Where'd you guys stay?" I asked.

Still catching his breath, Mark took a drag on his cigarette and pointed to a group of redwoods. "Over there by those trees."

Terra didn't seem so happy about the accommodations. She complained, "There's no water or anything, just a flat piece of dirt that we shared with the mosquitoes and ants."

I sarcastically said, "Putting it that way, You make it sounds really inviting."

"How'd you like the concert?" I asked Mark.

He enthusiastically replied "It was totally beautiful, man!"

"I guess this means you're glad you came!" I joked.

"Man, I didn't want it to end."

All I could say was, "I didn't either."

Terra was being noticeably silent so I asked, "Did you like the festival?"

She replied with a short simple response "Yeah, it was beautiful."
She seemed deeply absorbed with her thoughts and very distant.

Mark snapped, "She met some guy," then he added with an obvious sneer that he was unable to hide. "She's been like this ever
since." Sounding a little more like a twelve year old than a guy who
was at least twenty-four, he added, "I thought he was a creep!"

"No it's not like that," she defended. "We just talked. Besides,
you..." pointing at Mark, "...didn't even speak to him. I think you
would have liked him if you weren't feeling so damn sorry for yourself. There was something different about him."

Mark grumbled with disdain, "He seemed like any other guy to
me. Nothing special! Besides, I didn't think he was very interested
in talking to me."

I didn't want to get in the middle of anything but I guess the way
she was acting made me a bit curious, so I asked, "Why do you think
he was different?"

"This guy wasn't like anyone else I've ever met. There was something different about him. I don't know what it was. I just felt good
when I talked to him."

"I bet you did," Mark jealously responded. "And I bet he wanted
to feel good too."

In the short time I had known Mark, I hadn't seen this side of
him emerge. He was clearly jealous. I didn't know that he had anything more than a friendship with her.

She looked clearly annoyed. "What I was trying to say was that
there was...well, something different. I don't know what it was.
There was just something different about him."

Mark quickly lit another cigarette and snapped, "I didn't see anything so special about him. If you ask me, I thought he looked kind
of depraved," with a strained laugh he added, "...a little like that psy-
cho guy... you know, Anthony Perkins. He seemed to me like the
kind of guy who hangs out in dark alleys and school yards."

Terra ignored Mark and calmly said. "He seemed to be at peace
with himself. I mean he was happy and light hearted. He didn't take
things very seriously." She looked over at Mark and said loudly,
"Unlike some other people! This guy was funny; he made me really
laugh a lot. He said he's living in an ashram in Haight-Ashbury."

Mark was sitting with his arms and legs crossed, trying to ignore us, but it was more than obvious that he was feeling hurt and defensive. He started shuffling through his stuff and acting like he didn't notice us talking.

"What's an ashram?" I asked Terra.

"Well, I'm not sure. He said it was a group house where a lot of people live. It sounds like a commune. He said they're all into meditation, and there's this guy who lives there that he says is his guru or something. I don't know, but I thought I'd check it out."

Mark looked like he was burning with jealousy. He was the kind of guy that wore his emotions on his sleeve. He said what he thought and his personality didn't lend itself to subtlety.

Fascinated by the idea I asked, "Where is this place?"

Terra continued explaining, "He told me it's in Haight-Ashbury. He even gave me the address and told me to call him when I get there. You know, I can't say what they do there! Although I'm pretty curious too."

Mark threw in another wisecrack. "I think they're into white slavery. I think I saw something on TV about this. Yeah, I'm sure of it!"

I had to laugh. If Mark's hurt wasn't so real it would have been comical.

We all piled in the front seat of the van and were soon on the road again. Mark wanted to talk about the festival. He recalled each band and all the sights and sounds and all the excitement of the festival. He tried to remember every detail.

He said, "I've got some good friends back home who want to know everything. So if I go through this while the memory's still fresh, I won't forget anything. I learned this technique trying to study for school. I wish I would have brought a camera; because this place is beautiful. I can see myself coming back here someday."

I listened while gazing at the scenery along the road. Reflecting back on my own experience I remembered how the world looked so mysteriously beautiful. I had a new understanding of the workings of the subconscious mind and how we all cling so preciously to our egos. I had decided to keep my story to myself; it felt very personal to me.

We drove north to Santa Cruz past farms and miles of coastline and open fields. There was one more day left until Mark's flight departed for New York, and he wanted to be dropped off in Santa Cruz to see an old friend. He invited me to join them, saying that his friend was living on a farm where we could stay.

"Well, I don't know." I responded, "I really would like to get up to the San Francisco."

Terra looked a little alarmed at my resistance to going, "Oh, come on Trevor, what else have you got to do?"

Realizing that I didn't have any real schedule, I relented. "OK, I guess nothing. It's not like I know where I'm going or anything."

Terra smiled and let out a small sigh of relief that only I seemed to notice.

As soon as we got to Santa Cruz, Mark located a pay-phone and immediately called his friend. Terra and I wandered down the street to check out some live music. There was a jazz band performing in front of an outdoor cafe.

Before I had a chance to say anything, Terra opened up about all of the tension between her and Mark.

"Mark's been getting really weird since I talked to that guy. We were lovers one time...just once, and now he thinks he owns me. I never should have done it...not with him."

She paused for a moment while we walked. "That guy in Monterey was just talking to me. I thought he was really interesting. We talked for a long time while Mark was off, walking around and feelin' sorry for himself. At first I didn't even think that he noticed, but when he came back, he was acting all weird and jealous. I hate that kind of shit! I think he was expecting me to go back to New York with him. Shit, I got news for him! I only came this far with him because I feel like I owe him that, for all he's done for me."

We stopped to watch the Jazz band and Terra turned to me and asked, "Do you have a place to stay when you get to San Francisco?"

"No, I don't know where I'm going."

The closer we got to San Francisco, the more reality was setting in for me. I had no idea where in the hell I was going to stay.

"Well, I'm going to check out the place this guy told me about near Haight street. Maybe there's room for you too, That is, if you want to."

Now it was my turn to let out a sign of relief. "Thanks! I was just going to crash in my van."

"There is only one thing," she cautiously explained, "I don't really know what this place is all about. So let's just check it out first."

"That's OK, I've got nothing to lose. Besides I've been really curious about this place, ever since you first mentioned it."

She laughed. "I guess I noticed that."

We were listening to the music when a guy walked up to us. He was extremely thin, and his hair was stubbled, like it had been only a week since his head was shaved. With his drawstring cotton pants and bag, he looked like a Hari Krishna dropout. He approached me like he was going to ask for some change. "Can you help? I don't have any Earth-money, and I need to start raising some cash to feed the world's hungry."

"That is perhaps the most original approach to panhandling I've ever seen," Terra replied and reached in the pocket of her cut-offs and pulled out some change.

She said, "That sounds pretty ambitious but I think you better feed yourself first."

I don't think what she said even registered with him. She handed him the money and added, "Is this what they use on your planet?"

He just took the money and floated away talking to himself or to some invisible friend. Mark came up and joined us. He looked excited. "I got a hold of him. It's all set. he's only about four miles out of town. It's some kind of farm."

"That's great," Terra flatly said, sounding less than enthusiastic.

We found Graham Hill Road without too much trouble. It looked like a storybook, many of the houses lining the road had turrets, big gables and lots of wooden shingles. We passed a large grassy meadow that was surrounded by an ancient redwood forest. Some of the trees must have dated back over two thousand years.

"I've known Tom since I was a kid." Mark explained, "He moved out here about two years ago. I haven't seen him since. You know what it's like; we've been doing other things, but we were like brothers growing up."

"This is it," Mark said, spotting the address on the mailbox. "Go slow. Tom said there's all kinds of stuff to look out for around here." Just then a chicken flew right in front of the windshield.

We drove up a long dirt driveway with tall stalks of bamboo and lots of flowers growing along both sides. Another chicken flew in front of the van as we came to the top of the drive. Mark walked over to this old, wood shingled farm house while Terra and I waited outside by the van.

She said quietly, "I had a dream last night that I want to tell you about."

Before she had a chance she was startled into silence, "Hey, you guys!," Mark said.

"I'll tell you later," she whispered.

"I want you guys to meet my old friend, Tom." I thought Tom had a friendly appearance. He was the kind of guy you could trust.

"Welcome to the Farm," he greeted us like we were old friends.

"Is this your place? I mean do you own it?" I asked.

"No. Unfortunately, I just rent here," Tom said with a smile. He told us all about the farm and the countless varieties of flowers and fruits that grew there. He seemed proud of it as if, he did own it.

The farm stretched out over twenty acres, with shops for everything from fixing cars to milking goats. There were even a few artist workshops. Tom told us that the top of the hill was used for grazing the goats and smoking joints.

We hiked up a dirt path to the top of a steep hill, huffing and puffing all the way. The payoff was a fantastic panorama. I could see for thirty miles up the San Lorenzo valley, across forests of tall Redwood trees. Since there were no buildings visible, it was the same way it must have looked a thousand years ago.

Mark started telling stories in detail about Monterey. We tried to chime in sometimes, describing how Jimi Hendrix lit his guitar on fire, and the like but Mark's enthusiasm was clearly dominating the conversation. Then, Mark and Tom segued into old boyhood memories back in New York. They started gossiping about people that they knew from the "old neighborhood."

I sat and tossed rocks down the side of the hill and wondered if this conversation would ever end then Mark asked after they had run out of childhood memories. "So what are you doing these days?"

"I've been letting life teach me. You know, I'm just kicking back and trying to figure it all out. There's this group over in Felton..." He pointed out in the distance somewhere out in the forest.

"...They're teaching me about meditation and how to play guitar and I'm fixing their cars. I'm really digging it man. It's getting me high."

Mark sounding slightly cynical asked, "What do you mean? It's not like you're really getting high. Like pot!"

Ignoring Marks cynical tone, Tom said, "No, you're right. It's not like pot. It's not that kind of high." Tom looked up and with a renewed inspiration said, "It's more like feeling really good. You know how sometimes there just a perfect day when nothing can bother you. It's kind of like that."

Terra quietly said, "That sounds great."

"I don't know man...that's not like you. You used to be a party animal. Do you remember that time at the Mount Kisco Diner? Man, I've never seen anyone that drunk before. You actually threw-up on the table." We all laughed, "We had to carry you out of there."

"Yeah, that was a long time ago, you know, I was still a kid. A lot's happened. I feel like I'm at home here. I'm never going back."

Mark abruptly changed the subject, "Speaking of kids, did you hear about Frank? He married some chick from Yonkers, cause he knocked her up."

"No, I haven't talked to anyone."

"Yeah, and did you here that Vinnie got arrested for pot or something?"

Once Mark got started, there was no stopping him. He wanted to gossip about old friends. I was bored to death and even though Terra knew half the people they were talking about, she looked as bored as I was.

With Mark and Tom getting more absorbed in their conversation, Terra turned to me and whispered, "I want to finish telling you about the dream I had."

"Sure, what happened?" I said, not knowing why but feeling comfortable about Terra sharing this with me.

Terra looked to see if Mark noticed us talking, but he had launched into some memory with Tom about their first double date together.

"I've never had a dream like this before. It's really weird. I woke up from the dream really high. But it wasn't like drugs; it was better than that. Do you remember how I was this morning?" She looked at me intensely, almost like she was trying to psychically make me remember.

"Kinda." I tried to remember what I thought when I saw that distant look in her eyes this morning, "You mean the mood you were in?"

"Yeah, it's kinda like the mood I was in. Last night I had the most unusual experience. I had a dream I was in somebody's living room. It was an average living room, you know, a couch, a coffee table and a couple of lamps on either side of the couch. I was sitting on the couch, when this guy approached me carrying a tray. He served me a very elegant dinner. This guy looked youthful and somehow strangely very beautiful, with curly blond hair and bright blue eyes. There was something special about him. I can't put my finger on it. He just had this... quality. Almost like he was somehow more alive than anyone else.

In the dream, I said exactly what came from my heart I said, 'But I should be serving you,' and then he looked at me. His eyes had a compassion that was unworldly. He said, 'But you are my beloved.' I woke up then, feeling really high, like I had taken acid or something." She smiled broadly. "It was better than acid!" I've never felt anything like it before.

Mark overheard what Terra had just said and commented, "You were probably on acid and didn't know it. Maybe you were having a flashback."

Terra looked fed-up, like she had, had enough of Mark to last a lifetime. "No! I wasn't, you dumb-shit. I wasn't even talking to you. I didn't know you were eavesdropping!"

Mark looked as if he had been chastised. "I'm sorry. I wasn't eavesdropping." He answered defensively, "I just turned around and happened to hear what you were saying."

Terra tried to calm herself. "OK, just let it go." I know she was thinking to herself that she only had to put up with him for one more day. She turned to Tom, who looked pretty uncomfortable, and pasted on a smile. "This is a great place. How'd you find it?"

Tom looked relieved. He didn't seem like the type of guy that liked trouble. Maybe that is why he got along so well with Mark, who seemed to thrive on it.

"I just came here to buy some bamboo. Gus, the guy who owns this place, grows it here on the farm. That's when I met him. We got to talking, and I asked him if he ever rented any rooms. He did, and I moved in the next day. It was like magic I mean we got along beautifully. Gus is the coolest guy in the world; he doesn't judge anyone. I've really learned a lot from him. Not so much about farming, but stuff about life. He's friendly to everyone he meets, and he really loves sharing what he's got.

"I like the way he lives off the land. I'd want to buy a piece of land someday and have something like Gus has here. He hardly ever shops at a store. Most of what he needs comes right here from the farm. He gets milk from the goats, he grows more fruit and vegetables that he can eat, and he has chickens for eggs." Tom took a deep breath and looked around, "This place is paradise!"

Tom invited us to see the town, and treated us to a guided tour. We went everywhere from the shops on Pacific Avenue to Capitola Beach, where we stopped at a little restaurant by the sea. Isolated by cliffs and the sea, Capitola was a completely charming little town with everything from craft shops and restaurants to an old movie theater that sat right on the beach. We sat on a redwood deck that stretched out over the sand and had a perfect view of the ocean and Monterey Bay. I could hear the barking of sea lions out on the rocks. It felt wonderful being there. I didn't care what I ordered, I just wanted to sit there, feel the salty air and enjoy the peaceful rhythm of the Pacific.

Tom and Mark were still reminiscing about their lost youths while, and I let my thoughts drift away with the tide.

I was feeling both optimistic and anxious about Terra's ashram. I was curious but not sure if it was what I was looking for. I was hopping, I'd just know.

Terra had a strength that I trusted. She said what was on her mind with a blunt honesty. I wouldn't say she was a shy person, but she wasn't what I would call gregarious either. I really admired her qualities and wished I possessed more of them.

Maybe I would only be gone another week and then turn around and head home I rambled to myself. I wish that I'd see Laura again. I was trying to move on with my life but Laura was always there somehow. Always in my thoughts. At this point I just wanted to purge her memory once and for all. As much as I tried, her memory was still a source of pain for me.

A palm reader was walking from table to table and doing readings for people. I thought she looked interesting, even mysterious. She was a mature black woman with long hair that looked wild and free, like a lion. She appeared insightful with her deep brown eyes. Her Mona Lisa smile suggested that she knew something more and drew me in to find out what that was.

She asked as she approached our table, "Do you want to know what the future holds?"

Her eyes were deeply penetrating and soulful. When she cast her gaze on me: I felt even more confident that she could, indeed see my future. I don't know how, but I could always sense the intent of most people. It wasn't anything she said, it was in the way she spoke and the way that she looked at me. I sensed a kind of honesty that didn't care what anyone thought.

No one at the table spoke up. She was about to walk away when I sat up and asked, "How much for a reading?"

She smiled and said, "I charge five dollars for a short reading and fifteen for a full reading."

I heard Mark quietly snickering in the background. Then under his breath I heard him whispering, "I don't believe in that shit."

Ignoring him, I said, "I'd like a short reading. I can't afford much more than that."

Terra came alive and enthusiastically said, "Far out! Can I listen?" She was so sincere in her curiosity that all I could say was "Sure."

Mark stood up delivering a sarcastic attitude, as if he somehow knew better said, "I'm going to walk around while you see if you're going to get rich and famous."

Tom, patted Mark on the back politely chuckling and said to the fortune teller, "Don't mind him, he's from New York. We'll meet you back here," and they walked away.

"Mark's such an asshole," Terra said under her breath.

I was glad to have him leave. I'm sure he would have made it really uncomfortable by being rude the whole time. I was genuinely curious to hear what this woman had to say and didn't need any more of Mark's stupid wisecracks.

The woman took a seat next to me at the table. The restaurant was nearly empty; being too early for most dinners, but too late for lunch so we could proceed with some privacy. The palm reader sat quietly with her eyes closed, looking like she was quietly praying. Then she said, "The first thing I need to see is your palm."

"My right hand?" I asked.

"Yes...Yes, your right hand." She answered, with a distant tone.

I held my right hand out for her to examine. She took it and gently held it. She leaned down looking closely and occasionally touching different mounds on my palm. She turned it over and asked me to bend my thumb back. She studied it for several minutes, carefully examining all of the lines and crosses and touching it to see the depth and texture of the mounds. She never explained what the different parts of the palm meant or exactly what she was looking at.

After several minutes of examination, she let go of my hand and finally said, "I only use the palm to give me a guide to the personality and a timeline of possible events. The future is always being rewritten and your palm may change as you get older. I see it's a window to the soul." Then she started the reading.

"I see you're an honest person, and you don't have a lot of patience for people who aren't." She noticed Terra who was paying very close attention and asked "Is this your sister?"

"No!" I answered abruptly. "We're just friends. Actually, we've only known each other less than a week."

"Oh! What I see is that you have a close connection. It's like a soul connection. I believe you have known each other in a past life."

Terra giggled with delight. She was really getting into the reading; I'm sure she didn't expect to be included in such a way.

The woman looked at me again, with a bold directness. Her gaze had a precise focus. It was not necessarily a focus of the eyes, but a focus of the mind. I could feel her reaching inside of me.

"Do you believe in past lives?" she asked.

The idea of past lives wasn't a new concept to me. After all, I'm from California. I wasn't sure if I believed it, but I didn't disbelieve it either. I was always looking for some kind of proof.

"Maybe, but I can't remember a past life. If I could, then perhaps, I'd believe."

"Yes, I see you were together before, like brother and sister." She confidently stated.

Now that she had mentioned it, I realized that I did feel a kind of affection toward Terra. It was the type of comfort that comes with knowing someone for a long time.

"Something is going to happen..." She searched for words. "I can't see what it is."

With her eyes closed she repeated her words, "Something is going to happen, very soon."

I started to get worried and asked her, "What do you mean, is something bad going to happen? Should I go back? What's going to happen?""

Her eyes twinkled as she laughed. "No, I see you're searching for something. You've been searching most of your life but you don't know it. Your soul is searching. There's a great power to it."

She closed her eyes tightly for a moment. She looked like she drift into another world. After a few moments she dramatically let out a deep exhale, opened her eyes again and said, "I think you're going to find it."

She sat back in her chair and thoughtfully looked at both of us. "I'm sure you'll find it." She looked at me curiously and asked, "What are you looking for? because I get a powerful vibration."

"I don't know", I stuttered as I felt as my heart started to race, "I don't know. What do you mean, 'a powerful vibration?' I don't understand." I asked tried to sound casual, but only I knew my own underlying insecurity. "I think you're scaring me."

She laughed and said, "No, this is something very unusual. I believe this is a very good thing. I just can't imagine what it is."

"Is this something we're supposed to find together?" Terra asked.

"I don't know. Let me see your hand!" She took Terra's hand and looked at it for several minutes the same way she had examined mine. "I see the same changes in both palms. Perhaps you share this destiny. You see, the same vibration comes through both of you."

My mind was racing all over the place. I probably wouldn't begin to believe her had it not been for that hitcher back in Topanga Canyon. It sent chills down my spine just trying to imagine the possibilities.

I felt the same way I did when I was hit by a car as a kid. I was racing down hill on my bike, around a blind corner. There was a big bush that branched out into the street over the corner and I couldn't see any oncoming traffic. I was on a quiet country road and I had never seen any traffic before, so I raced down the hill as fast as I could. Before I had a chance to react: I broadsided a car that was making the turn. I remember getting up off the ground feeling stunned. I had no broken bones or anything, but I was shocked. I had that same feeling now.

"What's it about? Can you see that?"

"No, I have no way of doing that. Just trust. That's what you need to do. Keep an open heart and trust the Universe."

I knew she was right and I knew she was seeing something, but I couldn't imagine what it was. I almost wished I wouldn't have talked to her. I think it would have been easier not to know anything. Sometimes we fear the unknown a little too much.

She saw my reaction and said in the most reassuring manner, "Don't worry. I don't think it's time for you to leave this planet."

I sarcastically commented, "That just, really doesn't help."

She continued my reading, telling me about my nature and describing what my parents were like with remarkable accuracy. She even described events that occurred in my past. She even told me about a recent heartbreak and said that it will all seem like a distant dream very soon.

I thought she was an amazing person. I thanked her profusely when she finished. Then I reached into my pocket and paid for a full reading.

Chapter 8

Franklin

I pulled over into the departing passenger area of the airport and stopped the van. Mark seemed a little emotional as he directed his comments to Terra saying, "I know...I've been hard to get along with lately. Ok, I've been an asshole. I thought maybe we'd...well, I just think things have just been spinning out of my control." He touched Terra's arm and said, "I want us to part as friends. I wanted to be with you but now I know that'll never happen." Then he looked at her, scrunched his eyebrows, with a stressed expression and uttered, "I may never even see you again. I guess trying to hold on to you was like trying to hold on to the wind."

She laughed softly and wiped a tear from her eye. "But, you know the song, 'I may as well try and catch the wind'. We've been friends for a long time; I'm gonna miss you!" In that moment, Mark and Terra let their differences fall aside and gave each other a big hug. Although, I don't think Terra had any mixed feelings about Mark leaving; she was relieved to see him go. The tension between them was getting too overwhelming. I thought it was just a matter of time before they parted anyway. At times I felt so uncomfortable, if it wasn't for the promise of a place to stay, I may had left before Santa Cruz. I think it was better this way and besides, Mark had his life to get back to. I'm sure he was hoping that Terra would come back to New York with him. I felt sorry for him knowing how much it hurts to lose someone you care for. We said our final goodbyes and exchanged addresses, although I was sure that I would never get to New York.

Terra and I continued the final few miles into San Francisco. At one point the freeway rose above street level, and we could see the city stretched out before us. Unlike any other American city, all of the buildings are light in color, which gave the skyline a beautiful enchantment almost as if we were entering another culture.

We exited the freeway at Franklin Street and found ourselves suddenly in the midst of the fast paced commotion of big city traffic. Franklin Street was bustling with traffic and the blaring echo of irritated drivers blowing their horns. In spite of it, there was an irresistible excitement to this city; one I hadn't known. While chugging up Franklin Street, I prayed not to hit a red light. I wasn't sure what would happen if my van got stuck at a stoplight on the top of one of these steep hills. I wasn't sure if it would be able to start up from a dead stop.

The city looked different from what I had expected. The buildings were taller and the streets were narrower and more crowded than the streets of L.A. What surprised me most is that people actually walk. No one walks in L.A. It would never occur to anyone. I've seen people take a car to go two blocks.

Terra commented that San Francisco reminded her of Boston, but with lots of hills. I told her that I had never been very far from the California coast, and to me, San Francisco looked very cosmopolitan.

Terra reacted with some surprise. "You've never been anywhere! Wow! I've been around the world, probably a few times. My dad used to travel a lot for business when I was a kid. Sometimes he would take us with him. I've been everywhere." Then she started naming countries. "I've been to Italy, France, Spain, England, Japan, Korea, Australia…"

I interrupted her. "Do you see where we should turn?"

Terra stopped talking, suddenly realized that we didn't know where we were and started frantically searching the map. Occasionally, looking up to catch the street signs as we drove passed she suddenly shouted, "Turn left here! This is Geary Street. This is it!"

I hit the brakes, stopping abruptly, bringing traffic to a halt behind us. Almost immediately people started honking their horns.

I heard Terra say "Whoops! I'm not sure, but I think the sign says, no left turn,"

My hands were sweaty, and tightly clenched the steering wheel.

Beep! Beep! The horns were still blowing behind us. Someone passing on our right yelled, "Don't you know how to drive, you damn
hippies!"

"The light's yellow. Go! Go!" Terra yelled at me.

I raced the engine and popped the clutch, jolting forward, while
turning the wheel. I had to make a quick turn before the opposing
traffic hushed at us.

"Shit! That was intense!" I said with relief.

Terra started laughing. She put her hand on my shoulder and
started rubbing it. "You did great! I don't know what I would have
done."

After regaining my composure, we started talking and I asked,
"Why did you come here? It's not because of the palm reader?"

She didn't have to think too long before she answered "Well,
yeah that palm reader yesterday was pretty impressive but I decided
before I left New York. I was just drawn here. I never thought about
it. Something in me just knew I had to come here, this summer,
before it's too late."

I didn't ask but I wondered, 'late for what?'

Terra had an address that she scribbled on the back of a handbill
for the Monterey Pop Festival. We were somewhere in that area now.
Everything was so different from L.A. I was fascinated to see that all
of the houses were made of wood and looked like they dated back
to the turn of the century. I didn't see any stucco anywhere! I immediately fell in loved with the look of the city. I loved the old Victorian
homes and I also loved the way everything was so much greener. By
contrast, L.A. was built on a desert, the only time anything's green
is if someone waters it. San Francisco was naturally green from all of
the rain fall.

The homes were all flush against the sidewalks with steps up to
their front doors and no yards. Everywhere I looked all of the houses were stacked next to each other like dominos.

Without much effort we found the house, a big blue Victorian
mansion, three stories high, with gables on the roof and a rounded
turret along the front. It was beautiful. I parked in front on the
street. We both just stood for a moment; gazing up at the house and
wondering what future awaited us there. I worried that the guy she
met was only interested in her and wouldn't be too happy to see me.

Maybe they were into some type of a weird trip! I figured that I would just stay long enough to see if it was OK to be there.

Although I had been in a daze from driving; as we came closer to the front door, I was overcome with a sudden feeling of well-being. I was starting to feel as if I just woke up after a good night's sleep.

Terra looked at me, and in that moment, I saw what she was feeling without her having to say anything. I knew she was experiencing the same feeling of well-being.

As we walked toward the front door, she started talking about the guy she had met at the festival. "... we talked and hung out most of Saturday and I liked him. I thought Vajra was cool, that's his name, Vajra, he's the one who invited me. He said I was welcome to come and stay."

"What a name! Is he from the Middle East or something?"

"I don't know. He sounded American. Maybe his parents are from somewhere else."

"Are you sure if it's OK for me to be here?" I insecurely asked.

"I think so. He said the house was open."

A hand-carved wooden sign hanging above the door read "The way is Peace and the Road is Love." Terra knocked. It was oddly quiet for being in the city. All I could hear were some birds singing in the trees and a wind chime somewhere in the distance.

"Try it again!" I whispered to Terra.

She knocked a bit louder. No answer. I was starting to feel uncomfortable. I wondered if we had the wrong house. That wouldn't be a great scene: some middle-class housewife calling the police because she found two degenerate hippies at her door.

I suggested we take a walk and try again later, but Terra sat down on steps.

"You go ahead," she said. "I feel like waiting here."

I was much too anxious to sit and I wanted see more of Haight-Ashbury, so I told Terra I'd be back and took off on foot. It was only a few blocks down to Haight Street.

The street was narrower than I had expected. It was just two lanes with cables hanging above the center of the street for the electric buses. I hadn't seen anything like these since I was a kid. I think they took them all down in L.A. a long time ago. I heard it was to force people to drive cars, so they could sell more gasoline.

Every building was bursting with painted flowers and psychedelic colors that adorned everything. The storefronts looked as if they were built around the same time as the Victorian houses that lined the neighborhoods. Wood crafted designs protruded from every building façade, giving the environment a more festive look.

Haight Street was a confusing scene of tourists, hippies, and a lot of runaways. I was shocked to hear a bus driver giving a tour. It was like the jungle ride at Disneyland, "Just over on your left you'll see the famous 'Love Burger' sign; and just over to your right there are some actual hippies. Be careful! They may be on drugs." It was becoming a freak show for some tourist.

The runaways were everywhere and some didn't look any older than eleven or twelve, too young to be out on the street. I could easily see they were under age when they would walk up to me and asking for spare change. Everyone had a story. "I need bread for bus fare to get home," or "All of my shit was stolen."

As I wandered, I overhead some interesting conversations on the street. People theorizing about the nature of the soul or who's responsible for the war in Viet Nam. It was all part of the exciting tapestry of sight and sound.

I was looking for Sam and Silver, hoping I'd run into them somewhere on the Haight, but it proved to be like trying to find a needle in a hay stack.

Then there were all the tourists. I thought they were the weirdest. They were walking around taking pictures like we were animals in a zoo.

A very middle-class looking couple approached me and asked if I would pose with them for a picture. I think I must have been dizzy from all of the excitement, because without thinking I agreed. Before I knew it, this guy with a pencil protector in the pocket of his polyester shirt was standing next to me and his wife snapped a picture. I must have blended in pretty well, because they assumed that I was from the Haight.

"The folks back home are sure gonna get a hoot out of this!" he exclaimed.

I was starting to feel annoyed. I felt that I was being treated like a monkey at a zoo. I remember saying something like, "Where's that 'Animal Kingdom' guy, Marlin Perkins?"

The husband and wife traded places and this time she stood next to me and posed with her sunglasses hanging on a chain around her neck. The frames were the kind that turn up at the ends and were decorated with rhinestones. Pure fifties.

Her husband said, like it was a family picture "Now look at me and smile. One.. Two.. and Three.." click. I was getting more and more annoyed by these people. They never even made an attempt to talk to me. I felt they were being extremely condescending. Then the guy pushed his luck a little too far. "Oh, come on. Just one more picture. What do you care? Now this time, honey, look at the hippie. Now you, whatever you call yourself, look at my wife. One, Two…"

I'm still not sure what came over me at that moment. I knew he would snap the picture at the count of three, and just at that moment I threw my arms around her and laid a big kiss smack on her lips. A little crowd started laughing and applauding. The man reacted with shock that quickly turned to anger and within a matter of seconds into rage. He lunged after me, shouting, "You son of a bitch! I'm gonna kill you!" There was violence in his eyes.

Being at least twenty years younger than him, I was pretty sure I could out run him. I ran down the street as fast as I could. I could hear him swearing and threatening me as he tried to keep up. I was weaving around people, moving really fast and looking back when, suddenly I was yanked back by my shirt collar. A big truck came whizzing just in front of me. I fell on the sidewalk, stunned. As I laid there, I could feel the wind and smell it's exhaust fumes as it passed by.

Disoriented and confused I uttered "What happened? What just happened?" I didn't even know who I was asking.

A large black man leaned over me and asked with a genuine concern, "Are you OK?" I didn't immediately answer. I think I was still too disoriented.

"I'm sorry I had to pull you down like that, brother, but if somebody didn't stop you, you were gonna get hit by that truck." He knelt in front of me and helped me sit up.

"Oh my God, you just saved my life!" I looked at him in amazement. I repeated, "You just saved my life! You must be my guardian angel!"

He helped me to my feet and then put out his hand to shake. "Hi there, friend. I'm Franklin. What's your name, brother?"

I shook my head, trying to snap out of my daze. "I'm Trevor," and briskly, shook his hand "and I'm extremely glad to meet you. Very, very glad indeed. I'm sorry, what did you say your name was?"

"Franklin Roosevelt Jones. But you can just call me Franklin." He pointed down the street. "Do you want to take a walk? We can go down to Hippie Hill. You look like you need to sit down for a few minutes."

I brushed myself off. "Yeah, that sounds great."

Franklin was a tall man, maybe six foot, with a big Afro. He looked a little like someone from India with his loose-fitting Indian shirt and beads. He spoke in a soothing way, his voice soft, yet just loud enough to hear. "That was quite a scare you gave me. I was just out for a walk. I wasn't expecting to save anybody's life today." He smiled broadly.

"I wasn't expecting you to either. Say, that's a beautiful shirt you're wearing. Did you get it around here?"

"Yeah, there's a shop that sells these. They're from India." He looked at me. "You don't seem like you're from here. When did you get here?"

"How'd you know that I'm not from here? I'm from L.A. and I just got here!"

"He confidently stated, "L.A.'s a great place."

"You're the only one that thinks so."

We walked by a guy with a t-shirt that said, "No Turn Unstoned." I laughed and pointed it out.

"That's clever," He said. "I might have worn it at one time, but I don't smoke pot anymore."

"Why not? Everybody I know smokes some weed!"

He explained "It makes me feel too paranoid."

This was certainly not my perception of him. I couldn't help but notice that he had a sense of peace surrounding him, as if he had found something. You could feel a presence about him.

We were at a busy cross street and he said, "We're almost there we just have to cross Stanyan. You still look a little shaky. Be careful."

There was a lot of traffic and tourists gawking out their car windows. But like a true guardian angel, he made sure it was safe, walking slightly ahead and he put his hand out to guarantee that traffic stopped.

We walked a short distance to a grassy area that was known to the locals as Hippie Hill. It wasn't much of a hill. It was really more of a mound. There were lots of small groups of people making music and enjoying the sunshine. Some were even dancing without clothes. There was a 'free' feeling, where people weren't self-conscious.

We sat on the grass and continued our conversation. Franklin was calm and had a deep wisdom in his eyes. I was still curious about why he quit smoking pot and asked him about the last time he even tried it.

He knowingly chuckled, "I've tried everything. I even did heroin for a while.

"Yeah, but heroin's not like pot." I said, sounding like I actually knew what I was talking about.

He looked at me seriously. "I was really messed up. I was living on the streets after I got back from Nam. That war really messed me up bad. I spent two years there, two really long years."

"You were in Nam, man? What a bummer!"

"Yeah. When I got back, I didn't know what to do. I didn't have anywhere to go and no one to talk to. I couldn't hold a job; You know, I wasn't right in the head." He looked out at a group of teenagers, but his eyes were far away. "I saw things over there that no one should ever have to see. I did things that I'm ashamed of." His eyes started to fill with tears.

"Were you afraid?"

"Yeah! I was afraid. We all were afraid."

I was amazed that he was confessing all of this to me. It seemed so personal. I had never heard anyone speak so honestly about their experiences in the war. "Were you drafted?" I asked.

"No, I thought it might be OK. I mean I didn't have anything else going on. I couldn't afford to send myself to college, and they said I was only gonna be over there for two years." He looked down and shook his head. "Two long years in hell! A black man in the army gets all the shit jobs that nobody else will do. If you've just arrived, nobody even tries to remember your name. They call you 'new guy.' They figure you're not going to live long enough to bother with."

I didn't know if I should press for more. I was afraid that bringing back these memories was too painful for Franklin. Yet I felt that I owed him something, so I listened to what he wanted to share.

"They had me clean out tunnels. Do you know what I'm talkin' about?"

"No."

"The VC's", he saw my confused expression "..the Viet Cong, would dig out these tunnels underground to hide out in. They'd use them to hide ammunition too. So, whenever we spotted one, we'd send a man down to clean it out. 'Tunnel rat,' that's what they used to call us. Me and this other guy was the ones who usually had to go down. Most guys who have to do this don't make it out. I was one of the lucky ones. I'd have to go down there and shoot anything that moved. Sometimes they'd set traps for us. That's how most of the guys got killed. They'd trip a thin wire or something that would set off a claymore.

"I knew this one guy, Shamus, who just got to Nam. He was out on his first platoon and the sarge ordered him to go down. He had to do it. Man, there wasn't enough of him left to pick up.

"By the time I finally got back home, I was so messed up. I couldn't deal with it, any of it. I came here looking for some answers, but what I found was drugs. Not just smokin' pot, but real drugs, like heroin. I'd go down to the Mission district to score, and then I'd come back here for a free meal. I started doing that shit every day. I ran out of money and eventually ended up living on the street."

"How did you eat? What did you do?"

Franklin smiled. "Thank God for the Diggers."

"What are the Diggers?"

"People, real people. I don't know who they are, but I think they must be angels, man. Every day they come over to the end of the panhandle," he said, pointing somewhere behind us, in the distance, "and feed anyone who's hungry. They do a lot of good things around here. They even opened a store where everything's free."

"When you hit the streets, did you start shooting heroin every day?"

"Yeah, but I started in Nam. Everybody was smoking weed, and some of us started shooting smack. We were so scared all of the time that it was the only way we could get our courage up to go on. I even heard that the CIA was getting it for us. They'd do anything so we'd fight.

"After I got home, I thought I'd quit, but I couldn't. It just got worse. I started shooting up all the time. I was too embarrassed to tell my family. I didn't know where to turn. I wasn't even able to think anymore. There were voices in my head all the time, telling me what to do. Real voices. I could hear them. I was in constant pain. Eventually, I found myself thinking of suicide. When I wasn't high I just wanted it to quit so bad, and I didn't care how."

I was listening attentively. "But you're not like that now. What happened? I know we just met but that doesn't really seem like you. What changed?"

"I'm almost to that part. I eventually scored enough smack to kill myself. I figured it was the easiest way to go. You know, you just fall asleep and don't ever wake up. I was over in Buena Vista Park, leaning up against a tree. I had reached the point where I was ready to do it. I was ready to end it all. I sat there taking one last look at my life. I was remembering all of the good times when I was a kid, and I was thinking back on the things I had to do when I was in Nam. Then I heard his voice say, 'Stop feeling sorry for yourself. I've got a job for you.' I was stunned. Just a few seconds earlier, no one was there. I don't know where he came from.

"He was a young white boy, barely a man. He had clear blue eyes that were the picture of peace and compassion. He walked up to me, knelt down and put his hand on my shoulder and a feeling of peace washed over me. I felt clear in my head for the first time in years, maybe ever. I started to cry. I mean I was sobbing out of control."

Feeling touched by the memory, Franklin put his hand to his heart and looked at me. His eyes were watering. "My heart felt light and happy." He looked up at the sky for a moment. I could see that he was trying to find the right words. "No, I felt joyful. Completely at peace with myself. In that instant, he took away all of the pain that was torturing my soul." He looked right at me. "I know it sounds crazy, but I swear to you it's true.

I was fascinated and didn't want him to stop. I impatiently urged him "So, what else happened? Who was this guy?"

"You see, when he looked at me, I knew that he could see all of the pain I had been living in. Somehow he knew. He said, 'You weren't suppose to be there. It wasn't your karma to go. That happens sometimes.'"

"Had you told him that you were in the war?"

"No, but I was wearing my military greens. Maybe he figured it out, but I don't think that's it. You don't get it! There was something more going on here. Much more!"

I felt a little embarrassed for doubting him. "I'm sorry. I can be pretty skeptical sometimes."

"Yeah, I understand. I was always like that too. But his presence was so powerful that it just took away all of my doubts. You know how sometimes a person feels familiar to you? Well, I felt like I had known him my whole life.

"He told me he could take away that karma. I can't tell you what that means."

I was amazed by what Franklin was telling me, but I had never seen or heard anything like it before, so I didn't know what to believe. I didn't think he had made it up, but I wanted some kind of proof. I wanted to see this guy he was talking about.

Franklin continued his story. "The Master said, 'You're too sensitive. That's why you weren't able to cope with that type of karma. You've practiced meditation in many past lives."

"But how did he know that?"

"I don't know. He just knows things. He can look at you and tell you things about your life that you've never told anyone. I've been around him for the past year, and when he tells me about a past life, I believe him. He told me in my past lives I'd worked on developing a refined sensitivity. He said that in those lives, I was able to sit for hours in meditation, and now it's time to return to those karmas. He said that's where my strength lies. Then he said 'Come with me, and I'll help you'. I was cryin' like a baby, I was so relieved."

I touched his shoulder in sympathy, but my curiosity was still running wild. "Who is this guy? What's his name? Is he around here somewhere? I'd like to see him."

"I don't know what to call him, and I don't know where he's from."

I must have looked confused. "Did you ever see him again?"

"Sure. I just don't know what to call him. Whenever anyone asks, he just says, 'I have no name!'"

I was excited about the possibility of meeting this guy and asked "Is he from around here? Can I see him? I've got a million questions to ask."

Franklin held out both hands in front of himself and gestured "Slow down. One thing at a time. You stayin' anywhere around here?"

My voice lowered I was almost mumbling "Yeah, maybe. Someone's expecting me back. I should probably be heading there soon. Maybe I could catch up with you tomorrow."

Franklin calmly said, "Yeah, that sounds fine. Where are you staying?"

I couldn't find the address in my pocket. "I thought I had the address here, but I remember what the house looked like, and I remember what street it's on; down Haight and up Masonic."

Franklin got up. "I'm heading home too, and it looks like you're on the way. Let's go." He pulled out a pencil and a scrap on paper and scribbled down his name and phone number for me.

As we walked back toward the house, I told Franklin my story. I told him about Laura suddenly breaking up with me and about the psychic hitchhiker back in Topanga and the palm reader in Capitola. He listened attentively as we walked. I felt a little foolish after hearing all that he had experienced, but Franklin kept asking me questions. He seemed truly interested.

We also talked a little about the scene at Haight-Ashbury. Franklin seemed clear about what was going on in the Haight. "There's something very special going on here," he said. "It may just look like a lot of hippies dancing and taking acid, but there's a lot more. Just talk to some of the people, and you'll find that people are talking about deeper matters. That's the vibe here. Free love isn't just about sex; it's about the love of heart and soul. It's about sharing that love with everyone."

"They're doing that down in L.A. too, but not like here. I don't think people are getting it. They have this Hugh Hefner idea that free love is all about sex."

"Yeah, right. You got it!" Then he explained, like he was teaching a class, "There's always been some kind of bohemian culture. The beat poets used to gather down in North Beach. They were the hippies of their day. That's where the scene used to be, but now it's here. Right here in the Haight. I don't think it's ever happened to the level where it's become the popular culture before. This is something new, and it's spreading throughout the world."

He smiled knowingly, "But there's something else going on here."

We walked in silence for a while. Franklin interrupted the silence with, "This street, Haight, used to be known as 'politician's row.' It was before the big earthquake. This used to be where the rich and powerful folks gathered. That's when most of these Victorian houses were built."

I looked around, trying to imagine how it must have been. "It doesn't looks too rich now!"

Franklin said seriously, "This is a power place."

I had never heard that expression before. I curiously asked "What do you mean, 'power place?'"

A young woman skipped up to me carrying a bundle of flowers. She smiled sweetly, then picked out two roses and handed them to us. "Love is everywhere!" she said, and skipped on. I held the flower to my face, inhaling its sweet scent as I closed my eyes.

Franklin was in his stride and continued on with his lecture. "The Master, that's what I call him now, says there are different kinds of power places. L.A. is one. He says it's one of the best on Earth."

I laughed. "L.A.? Have you ever been there?."

He answered seriously, "L.A. is a place for dreaming. You can make your dreams come true there. That's why Disneyland and all of the movie studios are there. That's what the Master said. He said a lot of spiritual seekers have incarnated there."

"That's hard to believe. It just looks like a big, dirty city to me." I shook my head.

Franklin continued without any defensiveness that I could detect, "He said that a long time ago a race of warriors came to the shores in what is now Southern California and meditated. He said they were able to transcend this world, and they ascended to a higher existence. It left a charge on the land that is still there. People don't understand the power of that place, in the modern world and they misuse it, usually for their own gain."

"What kind of a place is this?"

He kept talking as we turned the corner "Oh, it's been re-awakening." I didn't ask him to explain.

He pointed down the street and asked how far I was going.

"Only a few more blocks," I answered.

As we walked up the street, I could feel a peace come over me. It was the same thing I felt earlier that day. I was feeling a calmness and a deep sense of happiness. When we got to the house where I'd left Terra, I looked at Franklin and said, "This is the place. I'll give you a call."

"Do you mean this place? This is the house?," he asked in amazement.

"Yeah. Is there something wrong?"

He was laughing, and I asked, "What's so funny?"

"I guess you found it on your own. Come on in. We're home."

Still laughing, he said, "I've been living here for over a year."

It took a second to register. Then I laughed and followed him. Franklin opened the front door said "What do you think were the chances of this happening?"

Chapter 9

The House

The front door opened to a narrow hallway decorated with beautiful original East Indian art depicting Hindu deities like Brahma, Hanuman, and Durga. They looked similar to the Indian arts I had seen at the L.A. County Art Museum. They were hand painted with exquisite detail. It was like a small, private gallery.

The end of the hallway turned into a stairway leading to the upper meditation rooms. Franklin slipped off his shoes and instructed me to do the same he just said, "We always take our shoes off."

To our right stood a large wooden double door; ornately carved with Hindu figures surrounding an OM symbol. I noticed that the walls and the molding were thick with layers of paint from many years of use. I asked if he rented a room there, but his reply was a cryptic, "Not really."

The door creaked open to a very large and empty living room. I followed across the bare wooden floor. I noticed that it was solid and barely made a sound as we walked. The lack of furniture was striking. Like the hall that led in, it looked more like a museum of Hindu art. Except for a stack of flat pillows the room was nearly bare. Unlike the paintings in the hall, these were on fabric. The only traditional piece of furniture I saw was a large armoire made of redwood burl. Its natural swirling patterns were beautifully highlighted with light and dark tones.

We walked through a door that opened into a spacious kitchen and moved through the kitchen without stopping. Except for noticing a lot of natural wood, I barely had time to see anything at all. I had a million questions to ask about the house, who lived there, and who owned it, but I thought it was better to keep them to myself for now.

I felt good. I don't know why, but I had the same sense of being refreshed and of well-being, as when we first walked up to the house. We entered what looked like another living room, but this one was much smaller and fully furnished. Terra was sitting and talking with someone on a couch.

"Trevor!" she shrieked, "Where have you been? I was about to give up on you!" Pointing to the guy sitting next to her, she said, "This is Vajra, the guy I met in Monterey."

I reached out to shake his hand and asked, "How did you like the festival?"

"It was beautiful, just perfect. Terra's been telling me about you."

"'Not much to tell," I laughed, then introduced Terra to Franklin and listened while he started to talk about the day.

"You won't believe what happened out there!" Franklin excitedly said. They both listened with interest while he told them the story of how we met.

"That's amazing" Vajra marveled, "I think Franklin must be your guardian angel."

"That's what I said."

Vajra commented, "It looks like you've come to the right place. Did he tell you why we're here?"

I looked at Terra to see if she had a clue what he was talking about, but she was focusing on Vajra and not paying any attention to me.

"No, I'm not quite sure." I shook my head and asked, "What you're talking about?"

Franklin answered a little defensively "Well, sort of... I started to."

"We're here to study with The Maitreya," Vajra explained. "To learn from him."

"Who's the Maitreya?" Terra and I asked simultaneously.

Franklin looked at Vajra with a little surprise. "You didn't tell her?"

"Well, sort of. I started to."

"What are you guys talking about?" I asked impatiently.

Franklin calmly explained. "The Maitreya, as Vajra calls him, is the same guy I was telling you about earlier. He stays here in this house, sometimes." He paused, thinking about what he just said. "Kind of."

"Not too many people even know we're here," Vajra added. "The Maitreya wants it this way." "The Maitreya is our spiritual teacher," Franklin answered cautiously. "But, if this is too weird for you guys, well, that's cool. I understand."

Terra sat up attentively. "Don't worry about us! We both know we're here for some reason. We just don't know what it is!"

Terra seemed surer of herself than I was. I didn't interrupt her, but I quietly held my own reservations.

"Where is he now?" she asked.

"I don't know," Franklin answered shrugging his shoulders. "He's not here that often."

"Where's he from?"

"We're not sure of that either. He just showed up one day," Vajra said. "Hanuman was there; he can probably tell you more when he shows up."

I started feeling confused, "Whoa! Wait a sec! Who's Hanuman, and how did he find the Master or Maitreya, or whatever?"

Vajra smiled patiently. "Hanuman is an older gentleman who owns this house. He lets us live here for free."

Franklin chimed in. "He even buys food for the house! He's into sharing what he has. He gives a lot of money to charities."

Vajra continued the story, "It was about three years ago. I don't know the exact date. Hanuman was taking a walk through Golden Gate Park. He said it was a clear evening, and he stopped to rest under a tree. He sat down on the grass to look at the moon. No one else was around. Something amazing happened. As he describes it, 'A cosmic wind came blowing through me.' Everything began getting brighter and brighter. He said the light was everywhere, all around him. It became so bright it was almost blinding. And then he described having seen the Master's image manifest fully in the light. He said when the light faded the Master remained standing in front of him. A human being. A God-Man. I'm not sure what to call him. Most of the time, he seems perfectly normal, but then he does something that completely blows your mind."

Franklin nodded in obvious agreement.

I was nearly speechless, "Wow!" I said, shaking my head. I could feel the power of the image that Vajra just described. Even if it's not true, I thought, it sure is a great story.

"When can we see him?" Terra asked with a genuine sense of wonder.

Franklin sat forward, resting his elbows on his knees. "Soon, I hope!"

Vajra went on, "Last week, the Master told us that there were several more people out there that he wanted to meet. He said it was our task to go out and find you."

I felt a nervous chill run through me. "Do you mean us? Terra and me?"

Franklin looked at me. "There were omens. Strong ones!"

"I felt drawn here," Terra explained enthusiastically, "I had a dream before leaving New York. Actually, I had a few dreams. In one of them, I saw a young man standing on a grassy meadow. He was wearing a white gown. He was completely innocent, like an angel. He reached out his hand to me, like he was inviting me to come with him. Then he smiled. Something happened when I saw him smile. I was filled with a kinda happiness. I woke up smiling. I swear it's true!"

"We believe you!" Vajra said with a smile, "We all have stories like that. I'll tell you mine sometime."

Terra continued, "A few weeks later, my friend Mark.." She looked at Vajra, "You remember Mark, you met him at Monterey...".

Vajra nodded in acknowledgment.

"Well, Mark told me he was going to California and asked if I wanted to come along. I had a really strong feeling about it. It's not like anything I can explain. I just knew I had to go. That's how I met Trevor. Shit! That seems like years ago. I can't believe it's only been a week!"

Vajra looked at Terra, smiled and said, "When I saw you at Monterey, I saw an image of the Master standing near you. I knew I had to talk to you."

"And I thought you liked me," Terra joked.

Vajra laughed. "Well, that too!"

"Is Vajra your given name?" I asked, feeling a little as though I was breaking into a private moment.

Vajra pulled his attention away from Terra long enough to

answer my question. "Vajra is a Sanskrit name. The Master gave it to me. He said I was a Sannyasin, or renunciate in a past life and that hearing my name might help me to remember that lifetime. He said I'd made much progress in that life and that it would benefit me to remember it."

"Has it?" I asked.

He laughed, "Not yet!"

I turned back to Franklin, "How come you don't have a name like that?"

He looked down and shook his head, "I don't know. I'm hoping."

Terra stood up and started pacing around. Vajra asked if she was feeling restless. She said that she was, and Franklin suggested a walk, saying, "It might help. This house is really charged with energy."

Terra commented, "No shit! I can feel it."

Vajra went over to her, directing his comments to her, "Let's go take a walk. I'll show you the Haight."

"The Master generates all of this energy," Franklin explained. "If you center it, you can have some very powerful meditations here. If not, it can drive you crazy. With all of this energy, you probably won't need much sleep while you're here. We only sleep about four to six hours a night. I'm not sure if the Master ever sleeps."

I asked, "Does he actually have a room here? This all sounds pretty mysterious to me."

"He stays on the top floor when he's here." Franklin thought for a minute. "I guess I can see how strange this must all seem. When I first got here, I was climbing the walls. The Master would look at me, and with the power of his attention, he could take away all of those anxieties. The anxiety you feel is, you fighting with yourself. You're trying to be something that you're not."

I shook my head in confusion. "How am I fighting with myself?"

"There's a calm center in the middle of the storm. You need to find that place inside yourself. You're used to always having some type of stimulation from the outside world. You know, something is always going on. It's either the TV..."

"I don't have one!" I interrupted.

Franklin kept talking. "...or the radio, or a record, or just always having to do something. Something so you don't have to face yourself. You told me about your girlfriend."

"My ex-girlfriend, thank you," I corrected.

He just kept on with his train of thought "...You see the thing that bothered you the most, after she broke up with you, was being alone. Alone with your thoughts and your desires, all gnawing away at you. But just imagine what you would feel like if you could control those thoughts. If you can control your thoughts then... bingo! You could stop the pain. What I'm saying is that, it only hurts because you think about it."

I was playing back all of these tapes in my mind about, what was going through my head just after Laura left. Suddenly, Franklin was making a lot of sense. He was nailing it, just as if it had happened to him.

"Your thoughts can drive you mad, if you let them. I know this because it happened to me. You've got to find your center. There's a calm center inside you. That's the way out of the pain. You gotta free yourself from those thoughts and desires."

"What's my center?" I asked.

"It's like your center of balance, but it's for your soul. It's even more important here because the Master has this house so charged with energy. It's like driving at high speed: You have to be more careful. It's important all the time, but it's more important while you're staying here."

"What do you mean?"

"Well, you know how those thoughts you have about your ex-girlfriend can really get to you? Let's say you found out that she's been sleeping with another guy. Or maybe she's been sleeping with everyone she meets."

"OK! OK!" I interrupted him, "I get the idea."

He laughed and said, "Maybe you're obsessing about someone that you wish was yours. No matter how you cut it, you're not living in the moment. None of these things are even happening. Or maybe they are. But that's a whole other story."

"What do you mean, 'or maybe they are?'" I asked, not hiding the hurt in my voice.

"That's gonna take some explaining," he said.

"I've got time," I replied flippantly.

He seemed like he was looking to give me the simplest answer, "Let's just say that you might be more psychic than you realize.

Sometimes when someone is on your mind, it's because that person is thinking about you. But that's a big subject, and I probably should-n't have even brought it up. What I'm trying to say is that she's prob-ably thinking of you. Maybe we'll get into it some other time."

"Should I call her?" I asked, practically jumping to my feet.

"No! Just let it go. If she tries to contact you, then you can deal with her. Otherwise don't think about her."

"But you said she's thinking about me!" I protested.

"You're missing the point. If you find her in your thoughts, then the way to deal with it is to recognize the source of the thought. Once you've done that, then you'll know it's not really you who's thinking it. Then it's easier to move on, you know, detach yourself from it." He shifted back to his previous train of thought. "What I was trying to say before is that everything speeds up around here. Think about what happened just yesterday. It probably seems like it was a month ago. Here, we find ourselves living in the present moment. So, it's important to be aware and try and control those thoughts. It's a discipline. Like working out. If you do it enough, it gets easier. The Master compares the brain to a muscle in that way. You work out, and your muscles get stronger. He said that if you learn to use your brain in different ways, you'll actually get smarter. He said science will prove it some day."

"How can I do all of that?"

"Learn how to meditate. Instead of always being focused on your obsessions, focus on your heart. If you focus on your desires, your desires will eventually consume you. Focus on your heart, and you will be consumed with compassion. It's a great high!"

"The Master says that if you stop your thoughts long enough, all memory of this world begins to fade. You enter into higher states of mind. You enter into samadhi. He says this is what happens when you die. There's love there! Real love."

"What's samadhi?"

"The best that I can tell you, since I haven't really been there, is that it's a state of mind that is beyond your normal perception." Franklin stood up and motioned me to follow him, "Come on! I'm hungry. Lets get something to eat."

He pulled some things out of the fridge and continued talking, "Have you ever practiced meditation?"

"Not really.", although I'd known about it for a while.

He took out some plates and put a few things in the oven to warm, then continued talking. "Meditation's an important tool, man. Most of the reason you feel hurt is because you're thinking about it all of the time. When you meditate, you learn not to think so much, or you learn to focus your thoughts somewhere else. The Master said, 'What you don't know won't hurt you.' All I can tell you is that it's helped me... a lot." Franklin made some tea and we sat down to a wonderful, hot vegetarian lasagna dinner.

"Who's the cook?" I asked. "This is delicious!", I said with my mouth full.

Franklin answered, pointing to his plate with his fork "Thanks, man. I made it. I've been learning how to cook. I've got some cookbooks, and I've been practicing. I'm going to try to start a business selling some of the things I make to some local health food stores. I think they'll be open to it."

"But, I thought Hanuman was paying for the food."

"The Master thinks it's good to work. He says we shouldn't feel bad about making money. He uses Hanuman as an example of what we can do if we have the money. We can help other people in need. I want to start making my own way."

"I never thought of it that way." I was touched by his wisdom. Franklin was probably only five years older then me, but he'd lived a lot more. He spoke with a maturity that was far beyond his years.

Before we had finished eating, I heard some keys jingling outside. My heart stopped. I was suddenly aware that it might be him. I don't know why I reacted so strongly. Perhaps it was all of the stories I'd been hearing. I didn't know what to do or how I should act.

I heard the door open. I didn't move a muscle. I didn't even swallow. Franklin looked a little nervous too. I didn't expect to see him react in this way. I heard some rustling, then footsteps coming across the front room. The footsteps were soft, as if someone were walking with bare feet. My heart was racing in anticipation. It seemed to take forever for whomever it was to reach the kitchen door.

The door pushed opened, and a young woman walked into the room.

Chapter 10

Suhalia

Franklin's shoulders dropped as he exhaled, relieving the tension he had been feeling, "Do you know where He is?"

She casually replied "I think he's coming here tonight. He may be along later."

I think my heart skipped a beat, just knowing he was going to be there. I don't know why I was so nervous. My hands and forehead were sweating as if I had been running. I reminded myself that I could leave any time I wanted; I could bolt right out the front door.

Referring to the woman I looked at Franklin and asked, "Who's your friend?"

Her soft cotton sundress flowed with each movement she made. I tried not to stare, but it wasn't easy! She was one of the most stunning women I had ever seen. Her long golden hair, copper tan complexion, and beautiful blue eyes took my breath away. She looked like she just stepped of the cover of a magazine. Something comes over me when I see a beautiful woman. It's like an addiction for me. I always start to idealize her thinking that she's the perfect woman.

"This is my friend Trevor. He's going to be staying here," Franklin announced.

She seemed to carry herself with complete confidence. While pouring herself a cup of tea, she said, "Glad to meet you."

Franklin introduced her. "This is Suhalia."

She smiling and immediately reacted, "Just call me Sue,"

"Did the Master give you that name?" I asked.

While sipping her tea, she calmly responded, "No. My parents grew up as part of the Lost Generation."

"What's the Lost Generation?"

"Oh, they were hippies before there were hippies. When they got a little older, they called themselves Beats. It's like a family tradition. We lived over in North Beach. They wanted a name that would distinguish me from all the Jane's and Jill's of the world. They thought Suhalia had an exotic sound; so I got it. I grew up a little differently from the rest of you. My folks used to smoke pot and take me to the Blue Unicorn coffeehouse, where they'd hang out and listen to the beat poets. I thought it was really boring, at the time, but now I appreciate it."

I answered with a fascination "Your name is exotic. It's beautiful."

She lowered her head slightly and softly said, "Oh, thanks." I could tell that she liked the compliment and was only acting shy. She put down her tea to cool and commented. "I'd love to get a name from Guruji, but getting a name is like getting a gift. It's something you can't ask for."

I shook my head in confusion. "Who's Guruji?"

"The Master," Franklin explained. "None of us really knows what to call him, so we call him a few different things."

Sue explained, "I asked him about it once. I said, 'What should we call you?' He simply said, 'I have no name.' So I've been referring to him as Guruji ever since. That's what they call a spiritual teacher in India."

"Sue lived there for about a year," Franklin added.

I could detect a distinct scent of the patchulli oil that she was wearing. It was sweet and intoxicating: my favorite. Now that I could see her close up, I thought she was even more beautiful. She looked about thirty years old to me. Her naturally dark eyebrows and lashes contrasted beautifully with her golden blonde hair. I found in her to have a strength of spirit that dominated the conversation. I think her strong confidence could be interpreted as being cold by some, but I knew it wasn't. I'm rambling, but I think you get the picture. I was quite taken by her.

"Are you going to be here for solstice?" she asked me.

I felt unprepared. "What is that?"

Franklin said, "The Master's been talking about it for the past two weeks. It's the first day of summer and the longest day of the year."

"He says it's the most powerful day of the year," Sue added.

I asked, "When is it?"

Sue answered, "It's the day after tomorrow. Or is it tomorrow? Either way, it's soon!"

"So, What's going to happen?,"I asked

Sue slowly took a sip of her tea and answered, "I don't know for sure. All I know is that Guruji has been talking it up for a while. He's been saying that this solstice is a special day and that he wants us all to be here. He said this year is especially important."

I asked who 'us all' meant. Franklin answered, while Sue went to the counter. She took an apple out of the wicker basket. I paid half attention to has answer, "There's only about a dozen of us. The Master told us that he didn't come here to teach this time. He said he's only teaching us because we were his students in past lives and he feels he has a karmic obligation."

"You mean he's been here before?"

"Lots of times", Sue answered. "But I only know of the few times he's told us about. I think he's as old as time."

She took a bite of her apple and continued. "I don't think you were here yet" she said, looking at Franklin, "but about two years ago Hanuman, Judy, and I took a long walk with Guruji down to the De Young Museum. It's a good ten blocks from here. There are a few benches that face the front of the museum. After walking, we stopped to rest. I don't know if you've seen the museum, but it's beautiful. With the tower, it looks like it's from another civilization or world."

"Guruji was sitting looking at the building and asked us if we remember any of our past lives. Hanuman and Judy both said no. I told him that sometimes I think I do, but I don't know if it's just my imagination. I asked Guruji, 'How can you be sure about something like that?'"

Sue touched her finger to a place on her forehead, between the brows and slightly above. "Guruji touched my third eye and said, 'I can help you remember. Close your eyes, clear your mind, and tell me what you see.' I closed my eyes and almost immediately I saw an image of myself sitting in a theater. The rows of seats were in a half circle ascending up from the stage. It sat under a dome ceiling that was supported by tall white marble pillars. The dome looked like it was white marble too. The whole building was white. I remembered it as clearly as something that happened last month. The theater didn't have any walls; the columns supported the dome. I saw The Master sitting in the middle of the stage.

As I was remembering this, he asked "Do you remember what you were wearing?"

Then he just said, "remember..." his words penetrated me. I saw myself sitting in a row of all women. We were wearing shiny black gowns. Then he asked, 'Where were you?' It came to me clearly. It was so clear that I could feel the humidity in the air. I said, 'Atlantis.' I was in Atlantis. I opened my eyes and said, 'There really was a place called Atlantis.'

"He instructed me to close my eyes again and asked if I could remember any more details. I quickly drifted back. I saw the temple and the people sitting there. It was like I was a spirit above the audience. I could see that the temple was built on the side of a cliff, surrounded by a forest. I had moved away from the temple to another building. I saw a women sitting, playing some type of musical instrument. She was touching these keys that were made of some kind of colored crystals. Unlike a piano, the keys appeared to be in a random order, and they were in different shapes and colors. 'I don't hear any noise,' I thought. Maybe it's not an instrument. What is it?

"After I opened my eyes, Guruji told me that the woman I had seen was accessing knowledge. She was tapping into secret knowledge that was kept in the machine. He said much of the knowledge of the past has been lost and wouldn't make any sense now, in these final years of this 42,000 year cycle. The absolute truth never changes, yet the details, the hidden knowledge, is in the astral realms. In Atlantis, we lived between the astral and the physical. We were able to easily travel between them."

Franklin and I were both transfixed. Sue continued. "I looked him in the eyes. I was in a state of near ecstasy. I said, 'That was you on that stage!' He nodded and simply told me, 'You've been my student many times before. That's why we're here now. Karma has a way of drawing us back together. You see, we still have some unfinished business.' When I asked him 'What unfinished business?' He completely ignored me and started talking to Hanuman. I didn't ask again. I knew from the way he reacted that it was inappropriate to ask."

Franklin cleared his throat "Wow! I've never heard you tell this story before. When did this happen?"

"About two years ago. I'm not sure." She took another bite of her apple, and asked me, "Are we scaring you away?"

"Are you kidding? This is amazing!" I didn't even have to think before answering.

We heard someone at the door again. This time I wasn't quite so nervous. Sue took another bite from her apple. She was so self-assured that I don't think anything could intimidate her. Franklin, on the other hand, sat staring at the door. He was clearly tense.

I heard the steps of two people coming through the front room. The kitchen door opened and Vajra and Terra walked in. Seeing Sue, Terra immediately introduced herself. Sue seemed obviously pleased to see another woman in the house and greeted her with a hug.

Terra, feeling much more at home said, "I'm anxious to meet the Maitreya," she said. "Vajra's told me some amazing stories." She looked around the kitchen and added, "I guess you've probably been doing the same thing!"

"No. We've just been talking about the movies. Did you ever get what Dr. Strangelove was all about?" I joked.

She politely laughed. "OK, wise guy. What really happened?"

"Sue was just telling us a story about something that happened a couple of years ago."

It didn't seem that Sue wanted to tell the story all over again, so she simply summarized with, "Sometimes being with Guruji is better than taking Owsley."

"We went down to the park," Terra said. "Do you know that there are people who live up in the trees?"

"They just sleep there," Vajra corrected.

"Isn't that dangerous?" I asked.

Vajra tried to explain. "It's safer, actually. That's why they do it. There are all of these runaways out there that are ripping people off. It's really a bummer!"

Sue sighed, "It wasn't like this a year ago. You should have seen it. It was beautiful! You could feel it while walking down the street."

I shook my head, "Doesn't anyone ever fall out of the trees?"

Vajra looked at Sue for confirmation. "I've never heard of anyone falling. Have you?"

"Not yet!"

I turned my attention back to Sue, "What was it like a year ago?"

"It was beautiful. It was like now, but without the runaways and tourists. It's still beautiful, but it was really pure then."

"The tourists are weird!" Vajra added.

Sue looked at Vajra. She spoke so quietly that I could barely hear her. "Do you think Guruji knew all this would happen?"

He shrugged his shoulders and shook his head slightly. "I don't know."

It was getting late, and it had been an extremely long day. This was a lot to absorb. I looked at Terra who looked like she was falling asleep on her feet.

Franklin noticed her too and said, "There's a big room upstairs where the women stay." Turning his attention to me at he said, "Sometimes the guys crash in the back room. We have a room upstairs, but it's small and pretty full right now, so you can crash here."

There was more Sue wanted to say. "I know you guys are tired, but I just want to finish the point I was trying to make. The first thing Guruji did when he got here was to do an empowerment. He said that this place was a dormant power place. He told us that one of his tasks was to re-awaken this as an energy center.

"You've been drawn here for a reason. There's a lot to explain before the solstice. I was hoping you'd be able to meet Guruji tonight. Maybe tomorrow. I know he's been expecting you both. He told us a week ago that you were coming. Our task was to find you once you got here."

I was suddenly awake. I looked to Terra for a feeling of comradery; she looked pretty alert again too.

"How could he know I was coming to San Francisco? I didn't even know." I asked, "What did he say?"

"He just said, 'I have a few old students that are on their way.' You both came with an abstract purpose. You were looking for something. Even though you didn't know what that was, you came anyway. Your karma brought you here." She smiled mischievously, "Neither one of you are tourists."

I was speechless. My head raced with anticipation, yet I felt a quiet excitement.

"Watch your dreams tonight," Sue advised. "We often have dreams where we meet Guruji. He teaches us in dreaming."

Terra and I were both silent but completely attentive "You see, in dreaming, Guruji isn't limited to having a human body."

Franklin touched the back of my shoulder. "I swear it's all true, man."

"How does he teach you in dreams?" Terra wondered aloud.

None of them could explain. Vajra honestly confessed. "It's something you're going to have to experience for yourself."

"Five minutes ago I was barely awake," Terra said. "Now I'll never get to sleep!"

One by one, everyone excused themselves for the night. I found myself alone in the downstairs level of the house. The solitude brought a feeling of tranquility. I walked out to my van to get my notepad and a few other things. It was quiet on the street and everything looked bright and shiny. The streetlights had a crisp clarity to them. I got the things I needed and headed back to the house. A thick evening fog had rolled in, and I could feel the cool, moist air on my skin. It felt good.

Chapter 11

First Meeting

I was returning to the house when I heard a voice behind me. "It's been a long time!" It was a disarmingly friendly and calm voice, with a soft resonance.

I turned around, wondering who could be there. Suddenly, out of the fog, a young man walked toward me. I wondered, 'Is this him?' But as he approached, I could see him more clearly and, although he fit the description with his shaggy blond hair, he seemed surprisingly ordinary. I thought perhaps he was someone else. Maybe another roommate living in the house or maybe just someone wandering up the street. He smiled and looked at me. As he drew closer I could see that there was something familiar about him.

"Do I know you?" I asked.

Suddenly I recognized him. He was the young man I had seen at the Dylan concert nearly a month ago. He looked strangely familiar then, and he looked familiar now. I don't know where or how, but I knew him. I'd seen his face a thousand times before. A glance from his eyes could fill me with a sweet gentle bliss. In that moment, I knew everything Franklin was telling me was true. I knew he was the one.

He approached me saying, "It's been a long time. I know you don't remember now; many lifetimes have passed, maybe thousands. Perhaps over time you'll begin to remember."

I was speechless. This was him! I had heard the stories, yet I secretly thought that much of it must have been exaggerated. If you want to believe something badly enough, you'll convince yourself that it's true. I felt comfortable knowing that I had reasoned it out, leaving my reality unchallenged.

All of that changed when he reached out his hand and touched my forehead. I was transported to some other place and time. I looked at him and saw the image of a large East Indian man draped in shimmering silk and adorned in gold jewelry. He was aglow in a vibrant golden aura. Then with a motion of his arm, I saw the young man again. He was calm and soothing like a gentle wind. He was detached and without fear. His voice was the pure sound of compassion.

I suddenly remembered seeing him standing across the street when I got hit by the car on my bicycle all those years ago. And I could remember him standing near me, when I was twelve. My closest friend had died in an accident, and I remember him standing near me at the funeral. I remember looking at him. He told me, "Don't worry." I remember how he made me feel at peace with my friend's death. I didn't have to cry anymore. I never questioned who he was at the time; I just remember his compassion.

Somehow I had forgotten all of these things, but they all came flooding back to me now. There were many more memories where I had seen The Master in my life. Always in times of need, he was there watching over me. I'd either see him in dreams or sometimes manifest, in the flesh. I never thought it was strange at the time. "How could you have been there all of those times?" I asked with wonder.

"Because I am not of time," The Master replied, smiling, "I have been watching you! We met a long time ago, in another life. Someday you'll remember."

My eyes teared up, and my heart was filled with emotion. I was completely overwhelmed by the bliss of his presence. This experience had affected me very deeply, I felt like I had 'come home.' I was surprised at the degree of my feelings. It was as if I'd been holding back my deepest feelings for a millennium, and now I could finally let go.

He touched my shoulder. "There's much to learn in this short time we have together." His words touched deep into my soul. I calmed down and was finally able to speak. We sat down on the steps of the house and talked for a short while.

The Master spoke to me with a familiarity "You were correct in following your intuition and coming here. You've already crossed the first hurdle. I called you here; that's why I've been expecting you."

"Me? You've been expecting me? I'm just a guy from the valley. I don't even have any spiritual background." I figured there must have been some kind of mistake.

He reassured me. "We've known each other in many past lives. There was a bond made between us thousands of years ago. A bond of teacher and student. I have a responsibility to guide you throughout your spiritual journey. There are many others, but few have been willing to follow their intuition the way that you have. There are thousands of souls that I've taught throughout time, but in this life there are only a handful of you who have been born here in America. A long time ago, long before this lifetime, I told my students that we would gather here in California."

As he spoke, I recalled a memory that was buried deep inside of me. I intuitively knew that I was having a memory of a time before I was born. I had a vivid memory of flying high above the city of Los Angeles, and The Master was there with me by my side. It was as if he was showing me where I was going to live. I saw the mountains and valleys. Everything on Earth was beautiful and alive with divine energy. I remember Los Angeles actually looking beautiful to me. It wasn't just the mountains or the ocean, but I could see an aura, a spiritual presence on the land.

"I'm sure by now that you are aware that I've been watching you and helping you for some time. I've called you here to witness and to share in this experience. This is a very special time for this country and for the world.

"Solstice is Wednesday. It's a very special celestial day. This year, in particular, is auspicious. It's the time when we begin anew. It's also a time when you can advance yourself spiritually. The energy is more conducive. That's why we're celebrating. There is something else that must be done at this time. There's an opening in the portal between the worlds. I see this as the omen that it's time to send a simple, yet powerful message to the world."

Although I was listening attentively, I was a bit overwhelmed with the bliss that I was experiencing in his presence. I felt at peace and had no need to speak.

The Master seemed to be aware of this and said, "Some of what

I'm telling you is at another level of awareness. You may not remember these words for years. I'm addressing different parts of your being. For now, just listen." He continued. "Most people think that New Year's Day is the time for making resolutions, but summer solstice is the real beginning. It's the celestial New Year. In past ages, people understood this and honored it, but this is the late Kali Yuga. This is near the end of the last age in the cycle of existence. People have lost touch with these natural cycles. There are four yugas: the Krita, Tretaa, Dvaapara, and Kali. Kali is the shortest in duration. It is so because of the deficiency of Dharma in the world. Hatred and anger are everywhere polluting our thoughts and deeds. Spiritual life cannot survive very long in this toxic environment. The Kali yuga has lasted for thousands of years. This may seem like a very long time; many civilizations have come and gone. Each ending with a greater loss of awareness about our place on the mandala of existence. We are now reaching the end of this age. The Kali Yuga is also known as the age of destruction, when a great purging occurs. This is necessary to cleanse the Earth. I'll tell you more about this. If you decide to stay," he said with a wink.

"In a few days, we will initiate the dawning of a New Age. This is not separate from the Kali Yuga but I see a time when the door is open. I see that a great opportunity for spiritual growth is upon us. This doesn't mean it will be easy. Sometimes when things are at their worst, we can make great leaps spiritually. Many of the early Christians experienced their highest moments before being executed for their beliefs. I'll explain more tomorrow when we are all together."

It was clear as he talked to me, that his knowledge was not of this world. His eyes looked distant at times, as though looking into another reality.

I saw another shadowy figure emerge out of the thick San Francisco fog. A slender older man about my same height was walking toward us. His white hair and beard almost glowed in the dim moonlight.

"Guruji," a mature but friendly voice echoed down the empty street.

"My good friend, I'm always happy to see you," The Master said as he walked over to greet the gentleman. "I'd like you to meet our benefactor, Hanuman" he said to me. "He is very wise, and he'll be able to explain much more to you."

Hanuman pressed his hands together before him in a prayer position, and then placed them firmly on the ground and knelt before the young Master. The Master touched Hanuman lightly and said, "I know your heart. You don't have to do that anymore." Hanuman stood, and The Master gestured with a simple motion for Hanuman to sit and join us on the steps.

Hanuman extended his hand to greet me, saying, "I am happy to meet you. Did you just arrive?" He spoke in a formal manner, like they did in the old movies. Like Claude Rains, with just a hint of a British accent.

The Master stood up and turned to go inside. We instantly stopped talking and turned our attention to him.

Speaking to Hanuman, he said, "Continue. Our young friend here needs to know as much background as possible before tomorrow. I'll leave you to talk. I need to prepare for tomorrow."

He took a step and then paused. "On Wednesday we are taking a walk through Muir woods. Solstice is coming and I think this would be a good place to meet." Then he opened the door and disappeared into the house.

Hanuman leaned back against the railing, "Are you here for solstice?"

I had been so high from The Master's presence that it took some effort to get grounded again and talk to Hanuman. "I wouldn't miss it for the world. What's going to happen?"

"I don't know, but I do know for certain that it will be good!" Hanuman seemed to perceive the difficulty I was having. "It's important to learn how to be focused for those times when you have to go out into the world. Otherwise I'm afraid," he said wistfully, "that people will think you've been taking LSD. When you leave this neighborhood that can be a problem. People won't understand you."

"How do you do that? I feel like I'm on acid now, and I didn't take anything!"

"For me it's not such a problem. I'm 77 years old, and I don't have any pressing engagements to meet. I'm set up pretty well here, as you can see. But you're still young. You're still going to have to face the world for many more years, and it's important for you to stay grounded."

I don't know if I could characterize Hanuman as having a glow, but I would say that he had a twinkle in his eyes, like a man much younger than his years. He had a relaxed and peaceful presence. I asked why it was so important to be focused.

"So you don't walk around talking to the trees," he answered. I laughed, but Hanuman looked serious. "I see this around here all the time. These kids are taking far too much LSD. They're losing their center. I say 'these kids,' because I'm old enough to be their grandfather. By taking all that LSD, they're doing damage to their subtle physical bodies, the bands of energy that wrap around us. It eventually puts holes in those bands. I see it all the time around here. It can take years to recover if they can recover at all. I've been told it's a great experience, but there are consequences. It becomes harder to focus on the physical world, and you need to do that to survive."

"How do I find my center?"

"Meditating is a good place to begin."

"How do I do it?"

"One way Guruji suggests is using a picture like a mandala to meditate on. I have one I can give you."

"You don't have to do that!" I answered instinctively. I was remembering all of times my parents told me that it's rude to accept gifts from someone you don't know.

Hanuman replied firmly, "I need to get rid of my belongings and I'd like for you to have it." This was an odd thing to say, but I didn't question him. "This particular mandala is hand-painted. It was smuggled out of Tibet a few years ago."

"Smuggled?" I asked, wondering if it was illegal like when they smuggle drugs across the border.

"Yes, these things had to be smuggled out. Tibet is closed to westerners. About seventeen years ago, the Communist Chinese invaded Tibet and over-threw its government. They've killed over a million people. Most of them being monks."

"I didn't know any of this. Was it in the news?"

"Not much. I suppose because there's no gold or oil there. But I wanted to tell you the history of this mandala."

"What is a mandala?" I asked.

"Most mandalas are simple geometric patterns. Some of them however, like the one I'm going to give you, are very colorful works of art. You'll understand when you see it."

"I don't even know where Tibet is."

Hanuman explained "It's north of India in the highest mountains in the world. It's the holiest place on Earth. I had some friends that were among the few Westerners to ever enter Tibet. They were there when the communists took over. They had to escape and they took with them several hand-painted mandalas. They are very precious works of art. They once hung in the great monastery at Llasa. My friend had to hand carry these paintings out of the country. He had to walk two or three hundred miles to India through the bitter cold of the Himalayas."

"How did he carry paintings for hundreds of miles?" I had a mental image this guy carrying several framed pictures over mountains.

Hanuman explained, "Many Tibetan religious paintings are on cloth scrolls. They're made that way because they're easier to transport. You see, there are no roads and no cars in Tibet, so they have to do everything by foot or on horseback. The one I'm going to give you depicts the life story of the great teacher, Lord Buddha. There are scenes painted all around it that take you through the phases of his life. In Tibetan Buddhism, they teach you to memorize every detail of the mandala and hold this image in your mind. Guruji says he taught this technique in a past life. This exercise will help you deal with all of the energy that he gives you. It will teach you to focus and help you keep your center. There are other techniques too, but this one is the simplest I know of. Do you know what I mean by 'center'?"

I wasn't sure. "Do you mean still being able to talk and maintain, even though you're really high?"

Hanuman laughed, "I've never taken any drugs. People of my generation didn't do that sort of thing. The others tell me that spending time with Guruji is much the same; they say that Guruji is a better 'high.' So I guess that's a pretty 'hip' description. But being centered means more than just being able to cope. It is maintaining your center of balance mentally as well as spiritually."

Hanuman reminded me of old Judge Hardy from the Andy

Hardy films, always calm and confident. Nothing seemed to rattle him. He told me how he began his spiritual practice at an early age.

"My mother had a great interest in anything mystical. She would take me to get my palm read or she'd take me to see different astrologers. Whatever it was that she was doing, she would always bring me with her. This was a very long time ago, and the world was a different place then. It was a much simpler world.

"I remember it was around the turn of the century when she met a famous Swami from India, Swami Vivekananda. I was only a young lad of eleven or twelve at the time. It's getting hard to remember. We had to travel first by wagon and then by train down to Los Angeles. There weren't any cars at the time; there weren't even paved roads. I remember the ride from L.A. to Pasadena more in terms of the dust on the road than anything else. When we finally got there, all I could think about was taking a bath."

I could see that when he spoke, the images were still fresh in his memory. Without explaining why he laughed, "That's just the way things were when I grew up. There were quite a few people there, but my mother was a persistent woman, and we waited until we finally got to see the Swami.

I approached with my mum by my side and she introduced me. I remember him very clearly. I can still see him standing tall in stature. He was a dynamic figure with a very bold presence. You would notice him when he walked into a room; he was that charismatic. My mother brought me down to Pasadena for the opening the Vedanta society. One day while we were there, I got a chance to speak with him one-to-one. I asked him if he would be my teacher. I remember what he said quite vividly, as if it had happened just last week. He leaned down and spoke to me in such a way that no one else could hear what he was saying. In almost a whisper, he said, 'Your teacher will come to you when you're much older.' After that, he treated me like the kid that I was, reminding me to do my homework. Twenty-four or twenty-five years later, Paramahansa Yogananda came to San Francisco. Have you heard of him?"

"I've seen his autobiography in the bookstore in Santa Monica. I read a few passages while I was standing there."

"Yes, he's the one. I thought maybe he was my teacher. He gave a series of classes in San Francisco and in Oakland. I could only go to a few classes. It was still much harder to get around in those days. Unfortunately, I didn't have an opportunity to speak with him. There were always too many people around him. I did hear him speak, and he inspired me to begin meditating."

We talked a while longer. There was something I had often wondered about. Normally this would be a hard question to ask someone so old, but I felt very comfortable with Hanuman. "Has The Master ever talked about what happens after we die? I'm sorry; it's just something I've often wondered about. No one teaches that sort of thing in school."

"They didn't teach it in my day either. Don't feel bad; it's something I've often wondered myself."

I apologized again for asking, and he reassured me, saying, "It's a good question. We're all going to die sometime."

Hanuman thought for a moment. "Ah, the bardo! I've read some about this. It's probably a better question for The Master. He once told us that after you die, you experience all of your karma. What that means is that everyone your life has touched, in any way. Let's say you're an evil person, and you kill someone. That person you've killed may have a family that depended on them for their survival. They may have a spouse, elderly parents and children who will suffer as a result of your action. He said that when you die, you will experience all of the pain that each of those people has experienced. Every bit of it. All of the grief in every life that has been affected by you. You will totally experience their agony.

However, your good karma can elevate you. He said you don't have to necessarily do anything great like finding a cure for cancer. He said it's more the little things you do, the way you treat the waitress at the coffee shop for example. Making an effort to just be kind to others. It all matters. You know, the times you've seen someone who's down and you give them a smile. All of those little things you do to help others. It all really matters. That's your karma. It's important to open your heart and find love wherever you can." He bowed his head in a gesture of devotion, saying, "Guruji is Love."

He put his hand out as if telling me to wait. "There's something that happened to me several years ago. I haven't told this story many times. Perhaps because most people wouldn't believe me. Several years ago I was visiting New York city. I was out walking through Central Park; I don't remember where I was going. I do remember that it was a beautiful spring day, and I was looking up at all of the colorful blossoms on the trees, when this loud, violent voice shouted at me. A man was standing about fifteen feet in front of me, pointing a gun at me. He yelled, 'Freeze, or I'll shoot!' I stopped right in my tracks."

I was intrigued by the calmness in the way he was telling the story. "Were you afraid?"

No, strangely enough. After the initial shock, I was quite calm."

"So what did you do?"

Hanuman looked at me very directly and said, "Something came over me. I wasn't afraid at all. I just stared at him. I looked him straight in the eyes. I didn't say a word. I think he must have panicked."

"What happened?"

"He took three point blank shots at me." He slowly gestured with his hand, like it was a gun, "Bang, bang, bang. All three shots missed. I heard a woman scream and turned to look. That's the last thing I remember. Apparently as soon as I withdrew my attention from the shooter, the next bullet hit me."

"It hit you? Where were you hit? What happened?" I insisted!

Hanuman looked up and recalled, "The next thing I remember was hovering over my body in a hospital room. I saw a doctor and two nurses packing up their medical equipment. They apparently had just pronounced me dead. There was some sort of clergyman sitting next to me. He was giving me my last rites."

"Were you dead?"

"Yes, but in an instant I was back in my body. I took a deep breath and opened my eyes. The words, 'I am the son of God!' burst from my lips. The people in the room dropped everything they were holding. I think the minister turned pale. He even dropped his Bible!"

"That's heavy! Did you ever tell The Master about it?"

Hanuman almost laughing nodding his head in a gesture of affirmation and added, "He said he sent me back to my body. I could never remember what happened from the time I was shot until just before I was pronounced dead. Guruji told me that he was there with me and that's why I'm still alive. He said I wouldn't remember until the time is right. He told me that there's a place beyond death where he can always be found. He remains there for us, even though he doesn't have to. If we meditate deeply enough, we can find him there even now. If we know how, we can travel there with no effort. And as far as remembering that time when I was dead, well, time is running out. I'd really like to know."

The front door opened, and we looked up to see Terra standing there, "Hi. Did you come out for some air?" I asked.

She looked a little surprised to see us both sitting there, and answered "Yeah, I couldn't sleep, so I came outside."

Her eyes lit up and she said, "Oh, you must be Hanuman," and she extended her hand to him. "I've been hearing all about you."

"And whom am I addressing?"

"I'm sorry," I said, coming to action, "This is Terra. We came here together."

"Is she your sister?"

Terra and I looked at each other and laughed. "People keep asking that, we're friends. We've only known each other for about a week."

"I'm sure you've known each other before," Hanuman said casually. "Well, I'm glad to meet you both. I hope this is what you've been looking for. Most people see Guruji and just see a person. They don't see anything else. I don't understand how that can be, but it's true. He walks these streets all the time. But you both seem to have some understanding of who he is. That's a good start!"

This surprised me, "How can they not see? It's so obvious."

I turned to Terra and whispered. "He's here! I talked to him about twenty minutes ago."

"Here?" she asked with excitement.

Hanuman spoke up. "He's gone upstairs; it's unlikely he'll be coming down again."

"Will I see him tomorrow?" Terra asked.

"Yes."

She almost leaped with excitement. "I have so many questions, like where did he come from?"

Hanuman looked pleased at the question. "I can't say for sure, but I believe he lives in a higher realm, what the Hindus call a higher loca. He says that he stays here, near this world, so that he can help others. He told me that in order for him to manifest in this world and take on a human form, he has to drop down several levels of consciousness. He said the ultimate enlightenment is void of all illusion, even that of power. It's a still perfection that lies beyond all of the boundaries of illusion. He says it's not perceptible. I think that's the best that I'm capable of telling you, having never been there."

Hanuman then stood up and put his hands on both of our shoulders. He spoke with the tenderness of a gentle grandfather, "It's getting quite late. Don't stay up too much longer. You'll need some rest." Then he went inside.

I had found something comforting about Hanuman's presence. He made me feel like everything was going to be all right as long as he was around. I knew I could trust him.

Terra and I sat and talked about all of the things that had happened. I was feeling a little overwhelmed. Terra confessed that she was feeling that way too. I thought maybe if I called an old friend like Ellen, it might help me to feel more grounded. Terra and I decided to take a walk and look for a public telephone.

We found a pay phone somewhere down around Ashbury. Like most public phone booths, it had a stench of human body odor and stale cigarettes. I was always afraid that I'd catch some horrible disease, so I'd brush my long hair over my ear so the phone never actually touched me. It was just a weird phobia of mine.

With a shawl wrapped around her shoulders to help protect her from the chill of the evening fog, Terra wandered up the street. I was a little concerned about her; she seemed vulnerable for the first time. She was more quiet than I expected her to be and a little spacey.

I found a dime in my pocket and called Ellen collect. She was the only one that I could think of that I could share my experience with. It was kind of late, but I felt like I needed to do this.

I dialed, Ring... ring...

A sleepy voice answered. "Hello?"

"Hi, Ellen, I'm in..."

The operator's voice cut me off. "I have a collect call for you from..." she said in a monotone voice, "caller, what's your name?"

"Trevor!" I answered impatiently.

"Will you accept the charges?"

"Yes!" Ellen answered, sounding more awake.

"Hi, I'm here! In San Francisco," I said with a high level excitement.

"When did you get there?"

"Early today. Although it seems like I've been here for at least a week. A lot has happened already."

"Well, I've been pretty busy too, since you left. This place has been like magic for me. But you go first. What's going on?"

"So much! I can't believe I was in Santa Cruz this morning."

"You were at the Monterey Pop Festival?"

"Yeah, but that's nothing compared to what happened after I got here." I tried to explain. "I'm not sure where to begin. I think that guy we met in Topanga, you know, that hitcher..."

"Yeah," she interrupted. "I still think about what he said."

"Well, he was right! There's something amazing happening here!" I think I must have sounded like a child after seeing a magic act for the first time, I couldn't contain my enthusiasm.

"Well, what is it? I know you're dying to tell me!"

"I've met a Guru! But that doesn't really tell you anything. That's just the tip of the iceberg. I've met someone who does wonders and embodies the source of all wisdom. I don't know exactly how to explain all of this. You have to come up here. I know you'll understand if you see him."

"See who? What are you talking about?" she asked.

"I'm not sure what to call him. He doesn't have a name." I felt frustrated because I knew that I wasn't explaining very well. I couldn't find all of the right words.

"Look, I've got a lot of things started here. I can't leave right now. You won't believe what I've been doing. The day you left, I set up my sewing machine and started making some samples, you know, of my clothing. I brought them down to this little shop called Threads in Santa Monica. Guess what happened?" She waited for me to answer.

"I don't know." My voice was flat. I wanted to share my new world with her but didn't know how.

"I only brought down four samples, but they ordered a dozen of each! They were two summer blouses and two halter-tops. I was feeling pretty confident, so I went out again the next day. I did the same thing: I took the same samples. I went to another shop, and I sold another dozen of each! So you see, I really can't leave here for a while. Maybe later; right now I'm just too busy. I've got all of this work to do!"

"That's really beautiful." I said. For the first time since I met Ellen, I felt a distance between us. I just couldn't connect with what she was saying. I was happy for her, but I felt like I was in another world.

"Laura called here looking for you. As a mater of fact, she's called twice now. I think she really wants to talk to you. Do you have a number I can give her?"

I couldn't get excited. I'd been waiting by the phone for so long, waiting to hear anything, just to hear her voice. I would have done anything to see her again, and now she was just a memory from somewhere in my past. Things that happened only a week ago seemed like they were a long time ago. I looked in my pocket and found the number that Franklin had given me. I thought about it, and then put it back in my packet without saying anything.

Ellen continued, "She wants to talk to you. I think she's feeling bad about the break-up. She said she moved out of her parents' house. She even has a new phone number. Do you want it?"

"No." I stopped to think about what I wanted to say. "I don't want to get involved. If you would have asked me a week ago, then things would have been different. I feel like I'm finally over her now, and I don't want to go back. I hope she has a happy life, but I don't know if I'm what she's looking for."

"What if she calls again?" puzzled with my change of attitude she asked, "What should I tell her?"

Feeling good about my response I added "Tell her I've transcended!"

Surprised she said, "Wow! You are going through something! I can hear it in your voice. You sound somehow clearer, like you're not afraid of anything. You really don't care if you ever talk to her again, do you?"

Then she quietly added, "Look Trev, there's something else I've got to tell you about. Two days ago I met someone. This guy walked into my life and I think I may be in love! I know what happened between us was very special and I'll never forget it but we were friends long before that night. I still want to stay your friend. You mean a lot to me."

Feeling a tinge of regret I said "As long as you're happy and it feels right then you should go with it. I always thought of you as a friend first. I don't see why that should change."

"Thanks for understanding. I guess that's the other reason why I'm staying here."

I saw Terra walking toward me, so I finished the conversation and wished her luck.

I got out of the stuffy phone booth. The fresh air felt good. Terra looked very detached, as if she was shielded from the world. I could almost see a protective aura surrounding her. She walked by everyone like she was invisible, just observing life and not interacting with anyone.

Chapter 12

Solstice Morning

I rubbed the morning blur from my eyes and looked around the room. It was about an hour before sunrise and in spite of the early hour, I felt surprisingly alert.

Franklin came bounding down the stairs and into my room, looking like he had already been up for hours. He greeted me with a big, friendly smile. "Good morning, brother". Feeling obviously exhilarated he added, "Today is going to be a great day."

He told me to go take a shower and meet him in the front meditation room. A few minutes later I saw Franklin seated on the floor. Upon hearing me enter the room, he turned and whispered, "Grab a pillow, and have a seat."

I took a pillow from the back of the room and joined him.

"We always do a morning meditation. It sets the tone for the whole day. Have you ever done it? Do you know how to meditate?"

"Last night Hanuman told me that I should focus on a mandala but I figure I'll just close my eyes and relax and that'll work too." I said.

"It's not exactly like relaxing. It's important to keep your mind focused on a single point like the mandala, but this is only one technique. Since we don't have a lot of time, I'll give you one technique that The Master taught us. He said to focus on a chakra." He reached over and touched my forehead. "This is where your third eye is. Focus on that point, and you'll learn how to see more clearly. Not with your eyes, but with your intuition. This will help you to open your third eye. Until the Master teaches you a new technique, I recommend you focus on your third eye. Whenever you catch your mind wandering, bring your attention back to that point. It takes a lot of work because while you're doing that you have to let go of everything else."

"Let go of everything else? How do I do that?"

"It's not easy, but you can slow down the thoughts that are always rushing through your head. Just do the technique I showed you and you'll see."

Terra and Sue came down the stairs and joined us on the floor. After a few minutes, Sue got up and put a record on the turntable for meditation. It was some kind of East Indian music, similar to what I had heard Ravi Shankar play a few days earlier in Monterey. It was transcendental and made it easy to get into a relaxed state. Then she opened the doors of the armoire. I was amazed to see several golden statues depicting Hindu gods and goddesses surrounding a large, ornate golden Buddha. The inside of the armoire was lined with a gold silk fabric decorated in beautiful Asian designs. It looked hand embroidered to my untrained eye. The Buddha statue sat on a golden silk pillow, and near the front of the altar, there were several candles sitting in brass holders, that looked like lotus flowers. Sue respectfully bowed at the altar, and one by one lit all of the candles.

Except for the music, there was a stillness present in the room. I heard a bit of shuffling and looked up to see Vajra come through the door. A fresh whiff of incense lingered behind him. He quietly helped himself to a pillow and joined us.

After only a few minutes, I noticed that Franklin was already sitting with his eyes closed in deep meditation. He seemed unaffected by the other sounds in the room. In his stillness, he looked like the picture of peace and perfection.

Then almost without making a sound, The Master walked through the same door and onto a small platform that elevated him just enough so we could all see him. In one graceful motion, he lowered himself into a half-lotus posture. Everyone around me bowed, so I followed suit. The Master looked at Franklin and quietly smiled; then he closed his eyes and, without speaking, he began meditating. I surveyed the room looking from side to side. Everyone had their eyes closed. Then I turned my gaze to The Master.

A golden glow emanated from his motionless body. This is something that is difficult to describe in limited human terms. His body appeared to sit in a state of suspension. I noticed that he wasn't breathing. He looked completely magnificent in his bliss. The entire room filled with the same golden luminance. I couldn't take my eyes off of him. It was clear that he lived in a realm of pure light, like nothing I could ever have imagined. You could feel the ecstasy by simply being in his presence. For a moment, I saw his body gradually begin to fade from view. I could see the pillow he had been sitting on, I could see the wall behind him, but The Master had vanished! I don't know if he traveled to another place or to another dimension outside of my perception.

I closed my eyes and easily drifted into a state of meditation. In The Master's presence, it was effortless. It felt as if his powerful presence pulled me into a very deep meditation. It left me feeling like I had been suspended in space. I lost all awareness of the ground below me and the room I was in. Time passed very quickly. Before I knew it, I heard people stirring. I slowly opened my eyes to see the young Master sitting before me. He looked other-worldly. His eyes had an indescribable shine and a distant look like nothing I'd ever seen. He was clearly absorbed in another reality yet still physically in our presence.

Sitting with The Master, I experienced a love that transcended human love. In my elevated state, I clearly understood that I was no different from anything or anyone else, and that this was the true definition of humility. I felt a deep respect and reverence for all life. I knew that the love I felt was a universal love, not the type of love we know here on Earth. It was a love free from the trappings of attachment, greed or jealousy. For the first time in my life, I felt complete.

"Today is very special." The Master proclaimed with a resonant and youthful voice. "It's a day of celebration and a day of initiation. Today is the beginning of summer, and I'm sending out a very powerful vibration on this day. This is not so much my decision; it's the will of the divine. It has to do with a shifting of energies. There's been a powerful planetary conjunction for the past few years, and all of these events are not by coincidence. My purpose here is to help direct the flow of this energy. I know there will be celebrations and observances throughout the globe today. With this sunrise morning meditation: We begin. The dawning of a new age is here.

Throughout this day, I will be sending powerful vibrations

through the lines of the world. These lines are luminous fibers that connect to every part of the Earth and touch every living being. I am sending a vibration using these fibers. These fibers are very real. If you could see them, you would see that they're really quite beautiful. As you learn how to access these lines, you can travel from place to place without effort. It's easier than thinking. You need to free your mind of the limitations of three-dimensional thought. It's all a matter of volition.

"There is a place. You could call it a state of mind. It's really more of an awareness. The place where the manifestations that you call miracles come forth. It's a place where the limitation of thought don't exist. Don't confuse the manifestations that you see with the Absolute or the state that is known as Enlightenment. Enlightenment is the 'stateless state', which lies beyond awareness. I am both an enlightened master and an occult master. I shift seamlessly between these states and non-states." He paused for a moment and closed his eyes.

Spellbound, I watched as his image, in a shimmer, became less and less clear. I saw the images of other beings standing behind him. They were beings of light. I psychically knew that these illuminated beings were there to help by giving their light and clearing all obstacles. The light around them became more pronounced, growing brighter and brighter until the entire room was filled with light. It was not like any light you could imagine; everything was illuminated, but there were no shadows. The light was everywhere equally, and it didn't affect the eyes to see it. My best understanding is that it was visible only to the soul.

The Master looked like he had taken on the form of one of those Hindu deities for a moment. I saw six arm with the hands held in mudra positions. The feeling of bliss in the room was intoxicating beyond anything I knew. In that moment I experienced a genuine love for all of creation. I knew in that moment, that we were really all from the one source. After a while, the illumination softened, and I saw The Master appearing solid once again and smiling. He interrupted the long silence and said in a soft voice, "Happy Solstice." Then he bowed.

We all sat in silence and waited for him to speak. I could see that daylight was shinning outside. The morning fog left droplets of water on the windows, making the light bend as it passed through a thousand tiny prisms. The silhouettes of houses and trees appeared smudged like a an impressionist watercolor, leaving only the shapes and colors for the eye to appreciate.

"Draw a deep breath," The Master instructed. I could hear lungs being filled throughout the room. "Now, just relax." We exhaled and let it go.

"Now exhale very deeply." He motioned with his hands, pushing down. We all did the exercise. "Push all of the air out of your lungs."

"Now relax again."

"When you inhale fully, you'll find that you naturally exhale without effort. Similarly, when you exhale fully, you will inhale without trying.

"It is in this way that we approach spiritual practice. You will find yourselves drawn to practice one of two ways. You will follow the esoteric path, or you will be drawn to the exoteric path. The esoteric path is the more internal way of practice. By avoiding all distractions, you find purity within. This is the way most people in the West approach spiritual practice. Through the avoidance of physical pleasures, you seek ecstasy within. You seek to unite with the divine within. There are some seekers who deny themselves wealth, sex, and even foods that excite the senses. They will spend many hours meditating and looking very deeply within.

The exoteric path is the more external. It is through looking at the world around you and seeing the existence of the divine within all things. On this path, you don't see the necessity of denying yourself experiences. You don't avoid anything. You seek to see the divine within those experiences. Nothing has a lesser or greater value, because you see only the divine manifest within all things. There is no need to avoid whatever experience life brings you. You may marry have children and become wealthy. It's all God. How can God not exist?

Living in this time, I think this is a more suitable way of practice. Celebrate life and celebrate the God within you and without you."

You see, like inhaling or exhaling, you are going to do the opposite without effort. So, I suggest Tantra. It is through the Tantric path that you learn to see the existence of the divine in all experience. Within you and without you. Which ever course you choose to follow will ultimately take you to the same place. All roads lead to Rome. Think about it.

The Master looked off into the distance, as if he could see far, far away. "I want us to go somewhere special today for the initiation today. I think Mt.Tamalpais would be a good place. It's a pure environment that is free from the distractions of modern life. An important tradition that we observe is the acceptance of some basic precepts. If you are willing to accept these precepts, and you are willing to live a spiritual life: I will initiate you as my student. If you choose not to do so, you may leave, and you will have my best wishes for a good life. I ask only that you tell no one about my presence here.

There are only four precepts that I ask you to accept for this first level of initiation.

• All life is precious. Respect all life understand that all living beings are from the one source.

• Generosity. It is through giving that we demonstrate our understanding of the spiritual quality that is inherent in all creation. It is how we share our light and help to elevate the lives of all living beings.

• Right speech. Through refraining from negative speech we purify our thoughts and deeds. This doesn't mean avoiding swear words: but avoid speaking of negative thoughts. Focus on the bright and light will find you.

• Meditation. It is through the practice of meditation that we may see and understand our own true nature. Need I say more?

"There are a few old monks who have joined us." The Master looked at me and then over at Terra. "Are you going to be coming with us today?"

Terra bowed respectfully. "Oh, Yes!"

I was feeling so overwhelmed that it was difficult to even speak. So I remained silent. I didn't know what the proper etiquette was.

I heard Terra say, "Yes. I'm very excited about being here!"

The Master joked with, trying to put us at ease. "Have Vajra and Franklin filled your heads with enough of their stories?"

Terra answered for both of us. "No, not at all!" Yet I was aware that nothing they could have said would have prepared me.

"I sent them out to find you. This was their task, and they did a good job. Wouldn't you agree?"

We both murmured a quiet yes.

"For his part, Franklin will be receiving a name today." I looked over at Franklin and I could easily see how thrilled he was with a smile that he couldn't hide "I think good work should be rewarded. And my friend Franklin has done an impeccable job. This task has forced him to elevate his awareness to a new level. I know that there are moments during his meditations when the world stops. This has been aided by his giving."

Speaking to Terra and I he said, "I knew you were coming and there are others still; their task was to find you and tell you about what we're doing here. I wanted you both to come here to be witnesses. Someday it will be important to tell this story. I don't know when, but I don't make these decisions. It's all God's will."

Just a moment earlier, I'd witnessed a miracle. I saw the room fill with a golden light and now he was speaking in a very normal manner. So much so, that he appeared almost ordinary.

The Master finished our meeting by saying, "Let's all meet there at eleven. Who knows where the meadow is?"

I heard a voice behind me. "I've made copies of the directions on the mimeograph machine." I looked over my shoulder and was surprised to see five or six people that I had never seen before. The meditation must have been so deep that I didn't hear anyone else enter the room. For just a split second I thought I saw Sam sitting in the corner. I had to shake my head and take a second look before I realized that he wasn't actually there.

The Master said, "I suggest the rest of you bring something to eat. We're going to be on the mountain for several hours." He gracefully stood in one simple motion and quietly slipped out the door.

Hanuman walked to the front of the room and passed out the directions. "You should decide who you're riding with. We don't want anyone left behind."

I felt like an outsider. I was the new guy; everyone else seemed to already know who they were going to ride with. Terra was talking with Vajra, and Franklin had already left the room. This was my first chance to spend some time alone since Monterey. The meditation had left me in a quiet, somewhat reflective mood, so I decided to slip away through the kitchen and into the back room. I thought I might riding alone and that would give me a chance to think about everything that was happening. I wanted to get out and see the neighborhood. I went to gather a few of my things and I was just about to walk out the back door when Sue entered the room.

"Well, I guess it's just you and me." She said, being the last person I would have expected to be without a ride.

I stopped in my tracks. "What happened to everyone else? Did they leave already?"

"Yeah everyone just cleared out. Do you mind if I catch a ride with you?"

Her presence made me a little nervous. I wanted to be her friend, but I couldn't look at her without imagining what the scent of her hair might be like or wondering how soft her lips would feel. These are the types of distractions that I was trying to avoid at the moment. I thought it was better to be detached, yet when I looked at her, all I could see was how she oozed sensuality. She must have been at least ten years older than me, and I think she saw me as a kid. But I couldn't help but wonder. I was also afraid of doing or saying something stupid and embarrassing myself.

I stuttered slightly. "Nnn..no, not at all. When do you want to go?"

"Any time. We have to stop and pick up some food. I know of a little deli along the way." Noticing my confusion, she said, "Maybe I can answer some questions that you might have. You look a little overwhelmed by it all."

I felt overwhelmed and even a bit paranoid. I wondered if someone asked her to talk to me. Then I watched a thought race through my mind: Did I look OK? I self-consciously combed my hair with my fingers, patting it down to hold it in place. But she didn't seem to even notice me. She just grabbed her purse and a sweater and started toward the door. "Where are you parked?"

I attempted to collect my composure. "Maybe I could use a cup of coffee. I'm parked across the street." I answered while walking out the door.

She put me at ease by telling me that she thought my van was groovy. I know this doesn't sound like much, but I was feeling insecure and grasping at any scraps I could get. I think she sensed my nervousness and made an effort to make some small talk.

Trying to put me at ease she asked, "Is this your first time in San Francisco?"

"Yeah, and so far I love it."

"Is this what you were expecting to find? Or is this all blowing your mind?"

At first I insisted, "No," then I immediately changed my mind, "maybe a little. I'm amazed and feeling a little strange too. I thought this sort of thing was only a myth. What about you? What do you think?"

"I always knew somehow," Sue thoughtfully answered. "I don't know how, but I just knew. Not that I would meet Guruji, but I always believed I would meet someone like him. I think this country is hungry for a spiritual awakening. I feel like we're all looking for something. Something sacred. I feel like I've found that. I'm not looking anymore."

We talked for a while. I began to see that she wasn't so intimidating after all and I discovered to my pleasure that she was even fun. She had a great sense of humor. I found myself feeling more and more relaxed in her company.

We drove through the city and over the Golden Gate Bridge across to Marin County. Right in the middle of the bridge, there was this sort of cloud hovering in the middle, like you'd expect to see floating past you in the sky. Just after crossing the bridge, the sun was shining again. Sue shrugged and said, "That's typical San Francisco weather."

My first peak at Marin County was of the beautiful, lush mountains covered with wildflowers. The highway curved up a steep grade; it really slowed down my little Volkswagen. I downshifted all the way to second gear. Sue was not paying attention to the car. "I know a place in Sausalito where we can stop. Have you ever been there before?"

"No. Where are we now?" I asked. We had just passed through a tunnel in the mountain and I was able to shift into third and then looked down the road.

"There's an exit somewhere up ahead. I think it's at the bottom of the hill."

I repeated my question. "Where are we?"

"This is Sausalito. It's a tourist place. There are lots of art galleries and ritzy places to eat here."

A beautiful red Ferrari zipped along beside us. I looked over, and I swear it was Grace Slick. She never looked at me though, she quickly speeded past us.

We stopped at a little supermarket deli and picked up a few things for the day: sandwiches, junk food, and two bundles of fresh flowers. As we were walking back to the van, Sue explained, "Flowers are a traditional gift that you bring your teacher. That's what they do in India. Today is an initiation, so we should bring these as an offering." She seemed concerned about me. "So, you must be wondering what you've gotten yourself into by now."

I'd had a chance to think and to be honest I was still feeling very overwhelmed by everything. I appreciated the chance to speak freely to her. "This is totally blowing my mind! I didn't know what I would find here, but this is outside of anything I could have imagined. Sometimes I feel like I just want to turn around and go back to the safety of my life in Topanga Canyon. It was a great life! Shit, I haven't even had a chance to see anything yet. Sue patiently listened while I kept ranting "I've heard about all of these people and things going on around here, like The Family Dog, the Fillmore, the Diggers and I want to see Stephen Gaskin, but things have been happening so fast. It's just blowing my mind."

"I had a feeling you were pretty overwhelmed. It's not always going to be this way. The Master has been talking about this since February or March. He wanted to use this summer; he said the astrology was right. He's usually not around this much. If you decide to stay, I can show you around the area." Before I had a chance to accept her offer, she added, "You know, you can do whatever you want to."

I found her offer to show me around reason enough to stay. Still holding the groceries, we stopped in front of the van. "I've thought of leaving, but this is much too interesting. I like it, but maybe I'm not the right one. I'm just an ordinary guy from the valley. The Master said that he's been expecting me, but maybe he's been expecting somebody else. Someone who's a little more spiritual! I don't remember any past lives and I've never even meditated!"

She looked at me and reiterated, "You're free to go at any time. No one is keeping you here. But I'm afraid," she smiled sweetly, "..that I'll be stuck in this parking lot if you leave right now."

She had an irresistible smile. I laughed. "No, I don't want to go. I'm just.. I don't know. This isn't what I expected. Maybe a better way to say it is that I never expected anything like this."

She laughed and touched my arm. "How could you have known? I don't know if anything like this has ever happened before. The Master doesn't come along very often, especially somewhere like America. He's come to Earth many times, but I think it's mostly in the Far East."

"So why here? Why now?"

"Did Franklin tell you how he arrived?"

I thought for a moment and remembered how he first came to Hanuman in Golden Gate Park. "Oh, yeah. How could I forget? Is that all true?"

"Oh yes! It's true all right. I've seen a lot of miracles since I've been here. Have you noticed how people all over the country, all over the world, are noticing the Haight? They are feeling the vibe. Have you ever wondered why?"

"Well, no. I just knew that this was the place to be. Everybody knows that!"

"How do you think that everybody just 'knows'? Guruji is consciously sending a message to the world from here. It's not the place that matters so much as it is the message. The message is that love is a better way. People, whether they know it or not, can feel where this is coming from. They can feel a higher vibration. That's why they're coming here."

As we continued our journey, Sue went on to explain. "Two years ago on solstice, the Master appeared before Hanuman in Golden Gate Park. Since then, he's been sending a message to the world. I think people are actually getting it!"

"What do you mean, 'he sent out a message'?"

"He's been psychically sending a message out to the world. I know there are people who will never understand, but many will. They're already beginning to. I'll spell it out for you. The message is about the way of peace. The path is the path of love. There are love-ins happening all over, not just in San Francisco."

"Yeah. I went to one a few weeks ago, in Elysian Park. It was really beautiful."

"It could eventually change world." She spoke with an innocent enthusiasm. "If we understood how love is the answer, there would be no poverty or war. I know I'm idealistic, but it's so simple! Over the past few years, Guruji has done several empowerments in the area. Tonight he is doing another one."

"What's an empowerment?" I asked.

She didn't have a lot of patience for explaining. I think she was frustrated with my questions. "If you decide to stick around, you'll find out." She pointed ahead.

"Turn off at the next ramp."

We turned off the freeway and followed the road as it wound past residential neighborhoods and then through the beautiful hills of the Marin Headlands. After a while, we turned off the main road and drove up through miles of winding switchbacks through a Redwood forest to Mt. Tamalpais.

It was a beautiful day. The sky was blue and the temperature seemed perfect. We drove with the windows open. Sue put her feet up on the dash, and I noticed her ankle length skirt slipping down, revealing her legs. She was truly a distraction to me. I tried not to look, but being only human, and I couldn't resist sneaking an occasional peek. I couldn't imagine how we could ever get together and I tried really hard to not even think about it. She didn't give any kind of indication that she was even slightly interested in me; I think she still saw me as just a kid, someone to mentor. Besides, Franklin had said something about everyone in the house being celibate.

The forest was thick with giant redwood trees. I noticed that when we passed under the shade of them, there was a big difference in the temperature. When I mentioned this to Sue, she explained that the trees were so tall and their canopy so wide that direct sunlight rarely reached the ground below.

As we neared the top of the mountain, we drove past a beautiful green meadow with poppies dotting the landscape. Sue lunged forward, putting both of her feet down on the floorboard. "I think this is it! Yes! This is the place. Pull over."

I pulled the van off to the side and looked around, asking, "Where should I park? Right here?"

"Yeah, I'm pretty sure this is it. We came here three years ago."

"But I thought he has only been here two years."

"Two, three, I don't know. I just remember being here."

At that moment, an old Nash came rattling up behind us. I could see in the rearview mirror that it was Vajra and Terra squeezed into the tiny two-seater car.

We parked, and the four of us crossed the narrow road together, walking over a small hill to a place in the sun. My backpack was heavy with food and soft drinks plus I was carrying a Mexican blanket I had bought in Tijuana. A few minutes later, Franklin arrived carrying a large ice chest. He looked like he was planning on a long stay. Just behind him were the five people I saw back at the house. I looked at Sue who was seated next to me and asked, "Who are those people? I haven't met them yet."

"They live together in a big house on Grove Street." Pointing them out one by one, she said, "That's Carlos, Sarah, Judy, and we call him Sun Bear, and she's Ritu."

"Did The Master give Ritu that name?"

"No, that's really her name. She was born in India. I really like her. I think she was my sister in a past life."

"Did the Master tell you that?"

"No, I just have a feeling. They usually come for the morning meditations and then leave right after. They've been with us for almost two years, but they mostly keep to themselves. I don't know; maybe they don't like us."

"Don't be so harsh," Vajra injected. "You're not always that easy to get to know either."

Sue tried ignored his comment. Judging from the way he snapped at her, it seemed that there was some sort of history between them, and that it was very unresolved. It seemed inappropriate for me to say anything, but it was starting to look like there was a tangled web of karma here.

"So, they don't live in the house?"

Sue answered, "No, not everyone lives in the house. It's just for those who want to be closer to Guruji."

They joined us and we all sat in a semi-circle, facing the Pacific. With the sun was behind us, we gazed ahead at what was a spectacular view of the mountain, as it gradually curved its way down to the sea.

Chapter 13

Initiation

The Master appeared radiant in his long white robe and golden locks gently highlighted in the sunlight. With his staff firmly in hand, he seemed somehow more regal. To me he was like a character from the Bible. I could imagine him pointing his staff and making the ocean part. He stood in front of our small group and smiled and posed the question, "Why do you think we're here today?"

Terra answered, "Because you're doing an initiation."

"Yes, but there's more."

Carlos spoke. "I think you're going to tell us some secret."

The Master just smiled. "Anyone else want to give it a try?" He paused, waited for an answer, but no one said anything.

"Today is the solstice. This is the day of greatest light on the planet. This is the historic time for celebration. When we were in Greece, we danced at Mt. Olympus to celebrate the light, the light that we perceived within all things. In ancient China this was seen as the changing of energies from the Yin season to the summer Yang season. In ancient Rome, we would celebrate at the Grove of Diana.

Solstice celebrations have been going on since humankind first became aware of our place in the universe. Today we're using this occasion to initiate a new beginning. We always welcome change and new beginnings. It's a chance to say goodbye to the past and to start over. Things will have to change. How that is done is up to humanity. We're here to celebrate the unlimited possibilities and the eternal hope that others will share in our vision.

"I came here for a specific reason. The world is at a point where it needs to make some decisions. Over the next thirty to forty years, humankind will collectively decide its fate. There are changes happening to the fragile Earth environment that won't be felt for another forty years. These changes will eventually touch everyone's lives. I've been meditating on the future, and I've seen many events that may occur; yet visions only give a view of possible futures. We have some choices to make."

The Master sat down in the center of the semi-circle and continued speaking. "You see this is an important time, it's still not to late. Humankind needs to start making some fundamental changes; changes in the way we think about our place in the cosmic order. I don't expect people to even think of it in this manner, but understand that we need to begin treating each other with an equal dignity. We need to go beyond the consciousness that divides nations and peoples and seek transcendence of these boundaries. It has always been the etiquette, of the enlightened to give warning. By sending this message at this time, I'm fulfilling that obligation. I'm giving notice to humankind with the understanding that there's still time to change.

"It's been only twenty-two years since the first atomic bomb was used. With this door open, there's been a race to create more and more powerful bombs. Right now, it's only between two countries, neither of which really want to use these weapons, but things won't always remain this way. Eventually these weapons will get into less stable hands. These weapons could be used to hold the world hostage. If we wage peace now we can avoid this potential future. The course of the future is not set, it can change.

"There needs to be a much greater awareness about the plight of the Earth. We need to realize that the Earth is alive; it's an organism. Look around and see the beauty of this world you're in. Learn from it. There is a perfection in nature. Learn to respect it and protect its delicate balance. A great deal of damage is being done to this planet with the motive of greed. The constant exploitation is eventually has an effect like a growing cancer. Leave it untreated long enough and the host organism will die.

"People have long felt free to use the resources of the Earth, but the numbers of humans will eventually overwhelm the capacity of these limited resources. The other creatures with whom we share this planet will soon begin to disappear. This is the canary in the coal mine. Pay attention to the signs.

"If we don't wake up we will fight one another for those precious resources. By the next century, the population of this world will more than double what it currently is. This will affect you both physically and psychically. I don't know if any of these things will change but if these trends continue at the rate they're going: I see we will have troubled times ahead. The Earth needs to heal.

"People need to learn the value of love. Real love, not attached human love. A divine love, a love that can be found within all living things. A love that we all share. This simple message can have a profound impact. We will not destroy that which we love. It's time to bring our hearts and minds back into balance. The power is yours. The decision is yours. I takes courage to love. It takes courage to recognize that this is your own true nature.

"Every year we do something special on this day. Two years ago I brought an empowerment from the other world, a realm of light and ecstasy, into this world. Last year we went into the street at midnight and brought forth another empowerment."

I was writing as fast as I could. Sometimes he took short pauses between statements, and I would use that time to go back and be sure I recorded everything correctly. I was so focused on my writing that I was having trouble keeping up with some of his thoughts. I apologize for anything I may have missed.

The Master continued. "I'm doing these empowerments for a reason. I want to send a simple message out to all who could inwardly hear me. By that I mean anyone who is capable of receiving this idea psychically. This is the way it's always been done. It's near the end of an age, and it's time to call on those who seek the truth. The simplest of truths is that we are all one, born of the one source. Everything else is illusion. Everything you think and all you touch and see will one day vanish from your perception.

"Although my message is simple, it could change the world. I don't expect anyone to consciously know where this message has came from. I have no self to care, no ego to please. It's enough to know that the message is about the way of love. The power of love is immense. It's the most powerful force in the universe. If we love our brothers and sisters, if we love the Earth, then things can begin to come into balance. If we truly love, we can do no harm. Love can put life back into balance. With love, we can feed the hungry. How could we allow those whom we love to suffer? With love, we can stop war. How could we do harm to those we love? I'm not saying this is going to happen, but with love, anything is possible. The world may never understand what we're doing here, but it's necessary to do it anyway. Remember, the way is peace and the road is love."

I found The Master's presence overwhelming. To sit in his aura was pure bliss. Dear reader, the best I can say is that we were transported to another world. It was clear to me that his world was a world without hate and violence. His message transcended all else.

"Later tonight I'm going to perform the last empowerment. My task is nearly complete." He stood and began poking his staff into the ground as he moved in a circle, he said. "I've already started, I can't help it. It's happening spontaneously."

"Master?" Vajra said, raising his hand. "Why is this your last empowerment?"

The Master stopped walking for a moment. "My task here is nearly done. I came here for one reason, to send a message, and that is nearly complete. It's like planting a seed; now it will take time to grow. We don't know if humankind is ready for this idea. Those who are less evolved will immediately reject it. Someday they will have to face that karma. When you turn your back on the divine you create a negative karma for yourself. I can only wish for all of mankind to succeed and hope that someday they will be free from illusion."

"Master, why don't you teach publicly, where thousands will see you?" Vajra asked.

"It would bring too much attention. Someone like me should never meet with the public. There are only a handful of monks that I'll meet with at any time. This is the way it's always been. It's rare that someone like me would even come here in the west. Because of the nature of my being, there is a very powerful karma involved in any interactions with me. You can make great leaps, or if you react negatively your karma will spin downward very quickly.

"For most people this lies outside their description of what's normal and acceptable. They have very fixed ideas about reality." He gestured with his hand like he was dismissing it all "It's all just an illusion." Then he just looked up and smiled again. "Usually I work only with monks who have spent lifetimes learning spiritual disciplines." He gestured like he was looking surprised to see us. "But in this life, I've got you!" We laughed.

"My message is simple, but very powerful. I see it as a way to avoid disaster. Without greater understanding, humankind will face certain peril. I come here as a deliverer of a positive message and also to give a warning that if this message goes unheeded, there will be a very powerful karma."He turned and sat down again. "There is something I want to talk to you about. There are things you'll need to know that will help you throughout your lives. A few of you are going to be here for a long time, and you'll need to know how to live in the world while maintaining your spiritual practice.

"By this I am talking about the secrets of the occult realms, a science by which you can better understand the inner workings of life. Be aware that these teachings are not necessarily the goal of the path, but rather a way that will help you better understand and deal with the world you live in. There are those who may not understand your spiritual nature. I'm going to give you a simple and practical description by which you can better see the world. This new description will forever change the way you see and relate to life around you. What I'm going to teach you is the lesser traveled path."

I wasn't sure what he was talking about. He was being more intense than I had seen thus far. He looked at each of us and said, "If any of you want to leave right now, I'll understand." He stopped and again, looked at all of us one by one and then seriously added, "If you decide to leave at this point, you take my love and my best wishes with you for your lives. Your lives will always be filled with grace. Does anyone have any questions?"

We were all speechless. The Master sat perfectly motionless through our long silence. His aura was ablaze, bathed in golden light. At that moment he was a million miles away. The power of his presence was the purest high I had ever experienced. No one spoke or even moved. I felt as if we were all of one mind and one thought. We all wanted to go on.

The Master opened his eyes once again and looked around; joking he said, "You're all still here! I thought you would leave!" We laughed. "Over the summer months, I'm going to spend some time teaching you how to become more psychic. This isn't to impress your friends. This is a tool for you to take with you and use to live healthier lives. You'll gain more power in your lives and have more control over your destiny. You need to become more aware of what people are feeling around you and how their thoughts can influence you. You also need to become aware of how your thoughts and your feelings affect others.

"Often when you have a conversation with someone, there are two conversations going on: the one that you can hear and the one that's being psychically or energetically transmitted either by you or the other person. You'll soon learn that people often don't say what they feel. You'll need to tune into this. Everyone is born with a sixth sense; it's a part of being human. The problem is that in modern culture you're taught from an early age that the world is flat. Through subtle messages from family and friends and the media, you're taught that thing are only as they appear to your five senses. Anything else is ridiculed. You eventually teach yourself not to trust your own intuitive understanding. So you shut it down. Now they've got you, you're now a consumer. The most magic you're likely to ever see is at Disneyland. I want you to re-awaken your intuitive self. Occultist are born not made.

"The first step is meditation. It's through the art of meditation that you learn to harness your mind. Normally you're probably pretty unaware of your thoughts. They drift from place to place like a boat without a rudder, just drifting whichever way the wind is blowing. You waste a great deal of power this way. Try and be more conscious. Just watch your mind for a while and see how many places it goes. You'll be surprised. You'll find old boyfriends and girl friends," he said, glancing at me, he said that, like he knew Laura was still on my mind. "or maybe you'll find someone there that you haven't seen in several years." He looked at Sue. She started laughing as if he had seen something she was thinking about. "You'll see that some of the thoughts you're having are not your own. They might be the thoughts of someone who is thinking of you, or you might be caught in a crowded place where you're experiencing the thought of other people who are physically standing near you. Either way it doesn't matter just stay mindful, and you will be liberated from the chatter. If you're aware of the source, you will have a greater level of discrimination.

"You live in constant illusion. This is your chance to free yourselves. What have you got to lose? You've got everything to gain.
Don't even look back.

"Once you've established a connection to someone, there's a line
between you. Similar to a telephone line; that person has your
number. They have access to you. By having this access, they can
have a modicum of control or influence over your thoughts. This
isn't anything to be afraid of. You should simply keep this in mind
while you're watching your thoughts. After you achieve some level
of mental self-control, you'll be able to follow these lines back to
their source and see who they are coming from. This is all a part of
being human the part they don't teach you in school. You will eventually be able to eliminate all unnecessary distractions.

"The sixth sense is the world of perception. It's not so mysterious
when you understand it. It's part of the inner workings and something you should be aware of. I'll talk about this with you more in
the future.

"You will learn to reach out with your awareness and easily perceive the vibrations of others. In Atlantis, a monk would have a
vision. He would see that a particular child was born, a highly
evolved soul. Usually the reincarnation of an evolved monk. He
would use his perception to find that child and bring them back to
the temple for training. I don't mean kidnap the child; the parents
would be thrilled to have their child learn the secret and sacred arts.
At that time they understood that this would be a benefit to the
whole family and that the family would prosper from make this
offering to the temple. This was also done in the high mountains of
Tibet until recently. It is a very long-standing tradition. If we could
find someone who wasn't influenced by the world and they had
already evolved spiritually in past lives, they would be easier to train.
It would be easier to teach them the art of 'seeing.' By the time they
were mature, they could be of great benefit to the community.

"This tradition doesn't exist here in the west. So it takes much
longer to bring you to a state of mind where we can begin. You need
to clear away all of your preconceptions and be aware of your
thoughts. Learn to become a witness to your mind. Whenever a
thought comes to you, look at it from a distance. Then look deeper

and see where that thought originates. In this case not who it's coming from but go to the source of thought itself. If you can realize this, you can see the source of all existence. You will awaken to a new understanding, to a cosmic awareness. The you that you think you are will no longer exist. You will see, understand, and become one with all things. This is the natural state. You will know that everything is born of God and always dwells within that place. The only separation is in thought or is in a clinging to a separate human awareness. Your true nature is God. The awareness of God, if you want to call it that. It's all God."

The Master instructed us to sit up with our spines comfortable yet straight and to practice being mindful. I put down my writing pad and drifted off into meditation. When I looked at my watch afterwards, I noticed that well over an hour had passed. It felt to me like it was only five minutes. I couldn't believe I was so anxious earlier. All of my fears and anxieties were gone now, washed away. All of my previous anxieties seemed like a foolish indulgence now.

At first I practiced the mindfulness that The Master had just taught us. I tried very hard, but it wasn't easy, so after a while, I let go and sort of flowed with the tide. I felt waves of different rays of light rushing through me. I could see an array of vibrant colors swirling around and through me. I had little or no conscious awareness. I was deeply immersed in a state that can only be described as the bliss of the soul.

At the end of the meditation, the Master stood and told us he was going to perform a very rare initiation.

"This is usually done with only very close students, but since we're here in America and you're the only students I have, I'm going to perform this initiation on you." We all laughed. "If you agree to the understanding that you will live a spiritual life and continue a practice of meditation, we will continue. This is the most basic precept."

I looked around; everyone was eagerly shaking their heads in affirmation. I looked at The Master and did the same. I didn't understand what was about to happen, but I knew I didn't want to leave.

The Master called us forward on-by-one. First he pointed to Franklin. Franklin was smiling, and I could see his eyes welling with tears as he stood up and walked forward. The Master took Franklin's head in both hands and pulled it to his own forehead so that the two heads were touching. He said something that I couldn't hear. I wondered if he was giving Franklin a name. Then Franklin stood up straight, and the Master touched his third eye. They were both silent for a few minutes, and then Franklin turned to sit down. It seemed like he couldn't see us or didn't notice us. He just sat quietly and looked contented.

Next The Master called Terra. She stood before him. Her back was to me so I couldn't see her face. The Master said something to her, and I heard her laugh. It seemed he talked to her for several minutes and then touched her third eye.

He pointed to me, and my heart skipped a beat. I stood up and walked forward. All he said was, "How's the writing going?"

"I think it is going pretty well," I nervously answered.

"Close your eyes now," he said softly. I felt his finger touch my third eye. I could feel his bliss pour through me. It spread through my being, like a warm glow of light, until I lost almost all awareness of having a human body. All that was left was light. I know of no other human experience to compare this with.

"Open your eyes now," he instructed. "Once you've entered the path, you will never be the same. If you should ever meet another enlightened being, they will see the mark I've left on you. They'll know that you have started on the path."

I bowed respectfully and said thank you and handed him my flowers. I felt like I was floating as I walked back to sit down. All of the things I thought of as important suddenly didn't matter. I had some awareness of my body returning, but nothing bothered me, and nothing could. The Master looked at me and said, "This is my world." I was perfectly content.

I sat in that contentment, wanting nothing, as the others each took their turn. We stayed on the mountain well into the afternoon and watched that glorious day pass. The Master talked to us for a while longer, but unfortunately my notes for those few hours are not as complete. I wrote only part of his talk.

After the initiation, the Master told us that we were now well on the path and the experience he gave us would always be there to guide us. He said we could draw power from it any time in our lives.

He said, "Everything...the Earth, the moon, the stars, every thought and every emotion that you feel and have all have arisen from the natural state. Even the light and the bliss that you've experienced here today. Remember to always meditate on the source; enjoy where it takes you."

He went on to talk about the need for a return to a greater spiritual awareness. He said, "People have become disconnected from the source and unfortunately don't know it. They go about their lives thinking that the circumstances that surrounds them is reality. Ultimately these things don't matter. The things you've learned, the jobs you've had, will all be forgotten. Death takes all that away from you; even your memories will fade. You will be left with nothing. If that's frightening to you, then welcome to the bardo. If you can embrace the nothingness, if you can let go of yourself then, welcome home.

"When this life is over, none of your friends can help you. I'll be your only friend. And what a friend I am! I'll just take you to some void and leave you there!" We all laughed. "I think it's time to get re-acquainted with God. What have you got to lose? Love is the closest word I can find to describe the divine, but even that is inadequate. It is the foundation of all creation. Without it we are lost forever in endless states of illusion."

He told us that we as a people were spiritually bankrupt. He said we need to bring these elements back into harmony or suffer the consequences. "There's a bigger picture than what we perceive. God knows no limitation, no time, or condition." He held out his hand and before our eyes, manifested a flower. "All things are possible when you are in resonant harmony with the universe."

The Master finished his talk and left the mountain with Hanuman. He told us to stay for a while and absorb what he had said. We would meet back at the house in the evening. I enjoyed the beauty and silence of the mountain and the feeling of the wind gently blowing across my face. After a while, I lay down on the grass and watched the colors of the sky and the clouds drifting by. I didn't feel like eating lunch or talking much, and I don't think anyone else did either. After some time had passed, Sue came over and whispered, "I think it's time to go now. Are you capable of driving?" I didn't answer so she restated, "Can you drive?"

I sat up and noticed to my surprise that everyone was gone. Sue looked at me. "How do you feel? Are you OK?"

"Yes, I'm fine. I'm better than fine. I've never been finer. I didn't realize what time it was." I must have seemed a little spacey. "I'm sorry. I didn't know everyone had left."

Sue laughed. "I didn't either. I thought someone would tell me."

I felt completely rejuvenated as if I had just had a perfect night's sleep. I didn't have my watch on, so I asked her what time it was.

"Relax," she said. "We have plenty of time. How do you feel? I know that was your first initiation." She calmly stated.

I felt really high in a way like I had never experienced before. I tried to gather my thoughts. Feeling dumbfounded all I could say was, "That was amazing! He's the real thing!"

I looked at her. "What about you? What are you feeling?"

"I feel profoundly moved. I know that I'm lucky to be a part of all of this. Guruji has taught me that nothing in this world is that important. None of the little things matter anymore. Nothing that has happened in the past really matters. All of our loves and hates just don't matter anymore. I don't know why I get to be part of this. I feel so fortunate."

"So do I!"

"I don't know why, out of the whole world, there's only a few of us. I want to go out and tell everyone I see but Guruji says not to. He said he's not here to teach the masses this time. He's here as a messenger. A messenger of the gods. I have to trust what he says."

We packed up our stuff and slowly walked back to the car. I turned to take one last look at the view, trying to remember how everything was. I saw the wildflowers and the blades of grass shimmering in the breeze. I looked up to see how the clouds looked. I wanted to remember every nuance and never forget this place. I wish everyone could have had this experience; it could change the world. Maybe even bring peace on Earth.

We were silent for most of the drive. I'd never been to the Marin headlands before, and I thought it was impressively beautiful. The rolling green hills, giant redwood forest, and cool ocean air seemed more radiant than ever. Eventually we reached the freeway, but this time everything looked different. It all had a shine to it. I wondered if this is what it looks like to Him. People were hurrying around, going about their routines, unaware that a strange and beautiful realm of ecstasy is just beyond reach.

As we moved into more populated areas, my mind became more restless. It was quiet while we were sitting with The Master, but now my mind was invaded by a thousand thoughts. They were mostly trivial things, like calling Ellen and my parents, or worries about money. I mentioned this to Sue, and she said that it was from all of the people living in the area and traveling on the freeway. I was picking up their thoughts. Sue explained that being in The Master's presence washes away your thoughts. She also pointed out that there were no other people up on the mountain. Now that we were back in the middle of a populated area, the impressions of others were all around us. The important thing, she reminded me, was to be mindful.

She put her feet up on the dashboard again, but this time I felt too detached to be distracted. She was explaining about picking up other people's thoughts. "We transmit our thoughts. People walk around transmitting, and everyone is doing it. It happens naturally, unless one is either enlightened or dead. You're like a receiver picking up all of these thoughts. Have you ever been in a crowded room where there are a lot of people talking, like at a party?"

"Sure, lots of times."

"Guruji used this example once. You know how you can start to have feelings, like desire, for someone who's there? It might be someone you would normally never be attracted to. You feel that because that is what "they're putting it out." It's a subtle message that says, 'Look at me' or 'Desire me.' Before you know it, you find yourself attracted. You're a good looking guy; you must have experienced this before."

I couldn't help but wonder if she was doing this very thing to me right at the moment, because I certainly found myself wanting her again.

"That makes sense to me," I said.

"Yeah." Then her voice dropped like she was embarrassed or trying to conceal something. "But he was trying to teach me to control myself. I'm a terrible flirt! He said it's even worse if you're aware of what you're doing. Oh, well, that's all you need to know." She seemed a little self-conscious.

Sue looked at me and continued to explain, "You're a prime candidate for being psychic." She laughed. She was starting to make me feel uncomfortable with the way she was talking. "Yeah, I think you're a prime candidate for this type of thing."

"Why's that funny?" I felt a little like there was some kind of a joke on me that I didn't understand.

"What I mean is simply that you're a very sensitive guy and you're more affected by all of this than you think. More than most people."

"But what do emotions have to do with it? I thought that was a distraction."

"No, not emotionally sensitive. Psychically sensitive. You're already psychic, but you don't know it. You have to develop it. You have to learn how to use it. Right now you're absorbing everything around you, and you're un-protected."

"What do you mean, I'm 'un-protected?'"

Sue thought for a moment. "You need to learn how to filter out the bad stuff."

"What bad stuff?"

"You know, observe your thoughts. If, for example, someone pops into your mind that you wouldn't likely be thinking of, that person is most likely thinking of you. Ask yourself are these the types of thoughts that you've had before? If not, they're probably not yours."

It was near sunset as we pulled up to the house. I knew there were only a few hours until we met again for the midnight ceremony. I wanted to shower and mentally prepare myself, and I had a lot of work to do on my notes.

I felt like the limitations I had felt my whole life were suddenly going away. I was free. I didn't know what was going to happen, and I liked that feeling. I had entered into a world of wonder.

Chapter 14

The Subtle Physical

With no time to lose, I absorbed myself in working on my notes, revising and recapitulating everything and making an effort to get it all on paper while the memory was still fresh. I was always careful to bring a few steno pads and several pens with me. It was all I could do to try and keep an accurate account of the dialog. As far as I know, no tape recordings were ever made. The only record of these events is either in the memories of those few witnesses or in my notes. One time Hanuman leaned over to me and asked if I was getting everything, so I assumed from his tone, that he approved.

Over the years, I had developed my own form of shorthand. My writing must have looked unintelligible to anyone else, but to me it was perfectly readable. Every slash and arrow meant something. Forever became 4evr and today was 2dy. It was my own written language and through years of practice; I was fluent in it.

The hour of our next meeting was upon us. Holding a feeling of adventure and anticipation, I joined the others in the living room for what I had expected to be an evening meditation to mark the end of the solstice. We were all seated on the pillows and waiting for The Master to come down from his room.

He walked in quietly, looking very impressive, almost biblical, wearing a full white robe and carrying a his long wooden staff. Without ceremony he stated, "Tonight is the last empowerment that I will perform.

"For the past few years there's been a movement of energy emanating from this center. I've been watching from a far for several years and now this remarkable movement has drawn me here, into this physical reality. My task has been to build this vibration to a higher level and make it apparent for all to see. I like what I see here. I even like the music." There was laughter.

"If I didn't do anything, this would all simply fade away and be forgotten. The Haight would just be another bohemian neighborhood and the world would never know the message. It is through the volition or the will of eternity that has compelled me to be here at this time. This movement that you have immersed yourselves in, has a spiritual foundation. I've been compelled to be here and give these empowerments. In a cosmic sense I've been invited. I don't have a choice; I have to respond. What you don't know is that this is rarely done in this world. It's usually not our business to get involved, but there's a lot of good that I see here. Young people are reaching for a higher vibration. In my world, this invitation cannot be ignored."

Vajra asked, "You used the words, 'usually not our business'. What did you mean by 'our'?"

The Master replied "I don't do this alone. There are many beings watching the planet. This is a rare moment in your history. A cosmic doorway is open. That was the invitation.

"I wish to provide a gateway for spiritual teachers to come here and help spread the Dharma throughout the West. It's time to begin a spiritual renaissance here in America and throughout the world."

"What's going to happen to the world? Will there be peace?" Vajra asked.

"That's up to humanity. After I've done my part, the collective consciousness of humanity will choose. Whether this message is accepted or not is yet to be decided. The decision is out of my hands. Humanity must either embrace or reject my message. The idea is as old as time, but it has being ignored and forgotten in this age."

There were moments in The Master's presence where I would see myself in another time and place. I saw myself in an ancient desert civilization and could feel the simplicity of that time. The walls would fade away and for a instant; I would see us all sitting together in a desert, listening to the Master speak. The image was strong and I would have to shake my head to try and snap out of it.

"What's the message?" Terra asked.

"It's a simple message, but a very important one. The way is love. People need to learn to love one another. From the poor and the disabled to the wealthiest among us. I use the word us because I am a part of you. Love can change everything. If we embrace this simple message, we can change the world.

"It's time to take care of the Earth. It's our home. It's our life support. Without it, we will perish. Its resources are not infinite." I felt he was being compassionate yet direct. "Tonight under the light of a full moon, we are taking part in this, the last and therefore the most powerful empowerment. From the occult perspective, the last is always the most powerful." I wanted him to explain more, but he simply went on.

"Why do we seek to be inaccessible?" The Master posed the question. He waited for an answer. It was quiet for a moment, and then someone behind me said, "I think it's to not attract any unnecessary energy."

"Yes, that's pretty close. When we draw unnecessary attention to ourselves, we often attract the ill judgments of others. People are quick to judge someone else. They may feel that they can elevate their status by looking down on another. This is a shallow way of thinking, yet you have all done it at one time or another. You're all guilty. That type of elevating of the ego actually hurts others. It comes from your insecurity and seeking the acceptance of others by projecting your dominance. Don't look outside yourself for acceptance.

"You need to rise above this basic impulse. Animals show their dominance by intimidating any possible opponents. When you choose to elevate yourself by belittling someone else, this only tells me that you have a low level of evolution. Instead, choose to look upon others as equals. You are no different from them. The same force that gives animation to life is within all of us.

"These types of judgments can affect the people you project onto more than you realize. If you become very sensitive, you can actually feel it. It's like something that attaches to you. If it happens to you enough, it can damage your subtle-physical body and affect your consciousness and your ability to meditate.

"People cast judgments for the slightest reasons; sometimes it's nothing you are doing but the way you look. Outside of the Haight, people call you freaks. It is a reflection of their insecurities and the lack of evolution of consciousness. People want to believe that they are superior in some way. The truth that they're no more important than anyone else is something that their egos will not accept. Your presence is threatening. There are people who have spent their whole lives carefully constructing a mental description of the world. Your expression of freedom threatens the validity of they're description. This kind of thinking leads to prejudice and, in those who are less evolved, even violence. When all else fails, there are those who try to enforce their control through violence. The graves of history are filled with the victims of this type of thinking. Remember that we all come from the same source; it is only our thinking that separates us. Beyond this is our separation from the absolute, the source of our unity. So rise above the illusions that separate us and recognize your true nature.

Unfortunately women are more often affected than men by the intentions of others. Isn't that right Suhalia?"

Sue looked surprised. I don't think she had expected to be called on. "Yes!" she answered. I'm sure she was wondering where this was going.

"If an attractive woman is seen on the street or just at a gas station, there are men who will leer at her. You might call to mind the image of the construction worker who makes catcalls at every pretty girl that walks by. Not to pick on construction workers, because unfortunately it's not just construction workers. It's men from all walks of life and in high places too. This type of thing has been going on for thousands of year. It's handed down from one generation to the next as if it were some sort of natural right that men should dominate women.

A lot of this happens on a very subtle level, they don't have to necessarily say anything, they just have to think it! Will it! Their intent, or volition is enough to carry an energy that slams into a woman. The fibers of the subtle or etheric body of a woman are not as dense as that of a man. This makes women very sensitive to these types of injuries. On the positive side, it's why women are inherently more psychic then men. This sensitivity is something that should be nurtured, developed, and protected. You need to be protective of your subtle-physical."

"What is the etheric body?" Terra asked.

"It consists of a structure of lines of which the physical matter of the body tissues is shaped and attached. The physical body exists because of it. It's really made of lines of energy. I see it as fibers of light. The etheric body is the basis for most medical practices in Asia. This will all be known in America too, someday."

What The Master was saying made me think of that Englishman, Pico, who I met down in Big Sur. He was talking about acupuncture using needles to move energy. Perhaps this was the same energy The Master was talking about.

The Master talked more about the plight of women in society. I sat there and really thought about what he was saying. I realized that I was guilty too. Maybe I hadn't made catcalls or acted in a blatantly disrespectful manner, but I would see an attractive woman and definitely lust over her. Sometimes I would look at a woman with a lustful intent and maybe feel envy, or anger, because I knew that she was unattainable to me, and she would never be mine. I saw that I wasn't looking at women as my sisters, but rather as something to have and possess. As I became aware of all of this, I felt deeply ashamed. This is not to say that admiring or noticing someone's beauty is wrong, but there is a big difference between simply noticing a woman's attractiveness, even with desire, and projecting an intent. For the first time, I saw where the line is drawn.

The Master went on to say, "In earlier civilizations and among many native tribal cultures recognized the power of women and elevated women to a higher position in their societies, particularly in their religions. I would like to talk about this some more. It's an important topic that affects half the world's population. We live in a world that is grossly unjust. This is a world where men are too often jealous predators and afraid of a women's power. It is a world where men try to dominate and control women. It is a world where men are often protected by other men and supported for their misconduct. This is unjust! We are all born equally from the same source. We should act with equal respect toward all children of creation. Sometimes change is painful but the outcome can bring great benefits for all. If men learn to let go, they too will be liberated."

He meditated for a moment in silence before changing the subject. "Right now we need to prepare for this evening. This is the end of the solstice of 1967; it is therefore the time of greatest power. By power I mean cosmic energy, the creative force that moves through us all. If we learn how to access this energy, we can more easily transcend this transitory world with its tall buildings and fast motor cars. You must let go of all of your concepts and illusions and let the cosmic winds blow through you and rearrange your consciousness. There's nothing to fear accept losing yourself.

"It's not necessary to draw attention to ourselves for what's going to happen next. I want you to 'hold in' your awareness. If you look at someone on the street, try focusing a few inches in front of them. Just enough so you don't quite connect. I want you to make yourselves inaccessible for tonight. We're going to go out to the street. Try and ignore any interference from people outside our circle. If someone approaches you, just be polite, but keep our purpose in mind. Don't waste your energy on trivial matters. Remember that we want to touch the world lightly. It's like walking on rice paper without leaving a mark. Because tonight is special and we don't want to attract any unnecessary attention. Besides, they'd never understand, let alone believe us."

We walked in a big group down Masonic to Haight Street, passing crowds lingering along the street. Everything looked to me like a black-and-white scene from a silent movie. The sights and sounds of the Haight were all around me, the people were animated but somehow hollow of substance. I was seeing life from a different state of mind.

Hippies were sitting around the street talking, and some were smoking joints right out in the open. I don't think anyone knew it was solstice, or even what that meant. As the Master walked past them, I was stricken by the knowledge that no one knew why this whole scene was even happening. To them, it just was. People were coming here from all around the country. I don't know why I had the good fortune to be here in The Masters company at this time. I had been going down the same road in life as many of these other people, but then something happened. A lot happened! I can barely remember my life in Topanga Canyon. Laura was just a memory from the past; when I thought about her, it seemed like it was just a dream. I don't even feel like I'm the same person that I was then. I don't think I'll ever be the same again.

I looked to my left and saw Franklin's gentle presence and realized how much his life had changed. I don't think he would have made it, if not for a miracle of fate. He has been transformed by his experience with the Master.

I see Hanuman walking before me, a kindly old man who's been so gracious in opening his house to a bunch of strangers. I know that he's been waiting his whole life for something like this to happen. In his East Indian clothes and long staff in hand; he looked like he was on a march with Mahatma Gandhi. He appeared old and thin, yet he had a youthful vigor like a man much younger than his years. I was impressed by his wisdom and acceptance of this new hippie subculture.

We walked a few blocks and stopped at the corner of Ashbury. It was fairly quiet, what I would call 'unusually' quiet. It was there that The Master gathered us in a circle around him. There were some people on the street but they seemed to ignore us. They just walked around us, going about their own business. I felt like The Master had done something so that no one would notice us. The world seemed unaware of our presence. On any other street in America, we would have stood out, but here on the Haight, nothing was impossible.

Chapter 15

The Empowerment

With his staff firmly in hand, The Master began pacing around in the center of our small circle. We consumed the entire width of the sidewalk. To my surprise, there was no one else around us. I don't recall anyone trying to walk around us or disturb us in any way. The Master continued circling and poking his staff into the ground with each movement. He looked at us and said, "Remember this moment. I want you to remember this moment." He kept repeating the same words over and over "Remember...Remember.."

As he walked I could feel the energy begin to shift. I could see a glow around him. I don't know, even unto this date, if anyone saw us there. With each circle he made, poking his staff in the ground, I could feel the level of divine energy accelerating.

Even though I was standing, I closed my eyes and began to meditate. I listened to his words. "Still your thoughts, and just flow with it. Let the energy move you and dissolve you. Tonight I'll meditate for you."

I knew he could generate such a powerful field of energy that it could wash away all of the chattering thoughts that I normally experienced. In his presence, there was only a blissful feeling of love. I opened my eyes to see him standing and speaking to all of us.

"Let your mind get kind of lazy. Just focus in a relaxed way." He started circling again. "Just let your thoughts go. Let everything go. You can't hold on anymore. Don't even try. Let it go."

With each word that he uttered, I felt myself gradually dissolve more and more. I felt the ecstasy and tasted a sweet nectar on my tongue. His words were all I could hear; everything else began to fade. I couldn't hold on to my thoughts any longer. My perception began to change. Everything started to take on a glow. I saw us standing in the circle from outside of the circle. We were all bathed in the same white-gold aura. It surrounded the circle and protected us.

The Master's robe looked luminous in the bright moonlight. I watched as he seemed to glow of a golden light. His staff looked like it had turned shimmering gold. The aura that surrounding him became brighter as I watched. He gradually became less and less solid. After a few more minutes, I couldn't see his feet touch the ground anymore, nor could I hear his footsteps. It's as if he was walking above the ground.

He was walking around and around in a circle with his staff, quietly repeating, "Love one another, and all is forgiven." I don't know what he meant by that; I don't even believe he was talking to us anymore. It sounded like a whisper from heaven. I kept repeating it over and over in my mind: "Love one another, and all is forgiven." I remember feeling that he was talking to the world on an inner level, beyond the physical. Beyond even words!

What I witnessed was unimaginable. I can only offer words, physical descriptions of what was of an ethereal nature, descriptions that can't possibly convey the wonder and pure majesty of this moment. He became an entirely different being. It was as if I had entered his world in some way. My perception had shifted to such a degree that I no longer was seeing with my human eyes but with my spirit.

"It's all love. God is love. Love is everywhere." He paused for a moment and then said, "This is the Summer of Love." I clearly heard him say those words.

He stopped and looked at all of us. "God's love is ultimately all there is. It surrounds us. We live in it all the time. It's the source of all inspiration. It's the muse. It's what you are. You just need to wake up and see it. When you cease to exist, it will be there to comfort you. It's there right now, and it always has been. Think of it as your lover who sneaks in through your bedroom window at night and seduces you. Tonight, I'm sending this love out to the world. It's time for the world to see that there's a choice. This is not my decision to make, but it's better to choose love. You see, my friends, we must seek to love and to understand our brothers and sisters throughout the planet, or we will perish. That's what's being asked here."

The Master told us to join hands in the circle. He put his hands together with his fingers pointing up in prayer position and stood still. He closed his eyes and chanted, "OM, OM, OM." As he chanted, his body became translucent. I could see lines of energy, like white light, stream forth from his solar plexus and streaming out in every direction out to the world. "OM," he chanted with a crisp clarity, his voice sounding gentle, yet strong. Afterward, we stood in silent meditation for a long time.

I never heard a sound on the street. I don't know what this all must have looked like. It was like we were standing alone. I felt transported to other parts of the world. I could clearly see the silhouettes of places like Stonehenge, the Acropolis, Mt. Zion in Jerusalem, the great pyramids, and many other places. It felt like we astral traveled to each of those locations and many more. It felt as if time had stopped and the world had stopped spinning 'round. I felt so good that nothing mattered. I was basking in the endless bliss of eternity.

The silence was broken when I heard The Master declare, "My work here is finished."

After a few minutes, I became aware of my surroundings again We were back on a street corner in San Francisco. Before leaving the circle, the Master made one more statement. We all gathered in to hear him.

"Remember the circle. The circle is tradition. It's the circle of life! We do this because thousands of years ago a race of great warriors came together like this to honor the light, to honor enlightenment. We do the same here this evening to commemorate and to honor those ascended beings. So we are gathered here, in this circle, as they once did to honor the God within. Our circle of light radiates outward from this point to influence others throughout the globe in the eternal hope that they will someday find liberation. It is always our most noble wish that all sentient beings find liberation."

He pressed his hands in a prayer gesture before him and said, Namaste, the Hindu word which translates to 'I salute the God within you'. We stood in silence. I can't tell you what an honor it was to be there yet at the same time I felt terribly unworthy. After all who was I to be standing in the presence of this great enlightened Master.

The Master started walking down Haight Street toward Golden Gate Park. Hanuman silently motioned with his hand for us to follow and then headed off in the same direction. We all followed. I walked quickly to catch up; I wanted to see how The Master interacted with people he came across and how they saw him. Would anyone see who he was? Or would he blend in without notice? We walked in a group behind The Master for the last few blocks down to the park.

I was walking just behind him with Terra to my right. I wanted to talk to her about how I was feeling and see if she was having the same experience.

The Master walked unassumingly down the street past several people, and yet no one seemed to notice him. I thought this was amazing. I wanted to shout from every corner.

I saw a man in a wheelchair on the north side of the street. He was carrying a cup that he used to keep change in, change that he was begging from people on the street. I looked at him and commented to Terra, "That guy must have some pretty bad karma. He must have done something pretty bad in a past life to have caused this to happen!"

The Master abruptly stopped and turned to face me. We all stopped, and everyone gathered behind me. The Master looked at me and said in an uncharacteristically harsh tone, "You don't know what his karma is!" I broke out into a nervous sweat. "This is not the result of bad karma or of having done something wrong. Sometimes bad things happen to good people. You only need to recognize the necessity to use whatever obstacles life brings you."

I felt deeply embarrassed. My face became flush and I think the hairs in my arms were standing on end.

The Master said, "The reason why I'm stopping you is because when you think those type of thoughts, you send a message to him. These are as bad for him as thinking racist thoughts about someone just because their skin is black. You can't judge from appearances; you have to look more deeply. Most of these souls out here are lost. They're in the place of the hollow ghost. The gentleman in the wheelchair has a very different karma." He looked at the whole group of us standing there. "You should understand this, because I've seen you all rush to judgment at one time or another."

The Master looked at the man and for a few moments, I watched as he sent a stream of light to him. The man in the chair started to smile. The Master suggested that we all pass by him and give him as much money as we could afford. He said we could use this to help cleanse our own karma.

Referring to the man again, he said, "It's a difficult karma to choose but it can be a fast path to follow. I can see that he is a seeker. He knows that his time is short on this Earth. With the advantage of having death watching you; you change the way you see life. Looking at him, I can see that this man has a degenerative disease and he won't live for too many more years. This is karmic. He needs to see that all of his desires and attachments vanish. He needs to see his life dissolve before his eyes.

In a past life, he prayed to Kali for rapid spiritual progress. She has answered his prayers. This will happen to all of you eventually with age. He's young and needs to learn to let go sooner. I'll help him!"

"I feel sorry for him," Terra commented.

The Master compassionately explained, "You don't need to feel sorry for him. He prayed for this life lesson. If you don't die a quick death, you will watch yourselves go through this same thing. You will grow old and feeble, and you will watch your body die. He's just on a faster schedule."

We walked across the street and each deposited some money in his cup. I gave him all that I had on me, about forty-five dollars. He smiled and said sweetly, "You must have all come here from heaven. Thank you." I could hear him shouting, "God bless you!" as I walked on down the street.

I didn't make any other comments, I just walked in silence for the last few blocks down to the park. We passed a big Victorian house on Haight Street that stood out in my mind, perhaps because it was the only house among all of the business storefronts. The door was open, and I looked in as we passed. There was a group of men and women of different ethnic backgrounds all sitting together, passing a joint between them. They were into a heated debate about the politics of the day.

I caught the eye of one of the guys there, and he held out his hand in a welcoming gesture, as if he were inviting me to join them. There was a genuine openness in his nature; it looked like a reflection of the vibe that was coming from The Master. I simply gave him the peace sign and kept walking.

As we walked along, I looked into the eyes of the people I saw on the street. I don't think I'd ever seen this before, but there was an emptiness of spirit in many of the faces. It looked like they were all longing for something. Although, I'm sure they didn't see themselves this way, I did. In my elevated state of awareness, I could see the emptiness of their souls. I know they never would have imagined that the answer to all of their deepest longings was walking right past them on the street, undetected.

We crossed Stanyon and hiked pretty far through the park. We must have gone fifteen or twenty blocks. Passing lots of trees and meadows, passed hippie hill, passed the Botanical Gardens and Stow Lake and finally came to a little lake with no roads around it. I think we were on the outskirts of 23rd or 24th street. With his fast and steady gate, The Master was difficult to keep up with. I don't know how Hanuman managed, but he seemed to be doing better than me. I never saw him stop to rest or even catch his breath. It was clear that he was in better shape than myself; who, at twenty, needed to stop and rest.

There was a stillness in the air, the kind of stillness that is so quiet that every sound stands out against the background of silence, every squirrel hopping about and every leaf that touched the ground. The moonlight was bright enough to fill the sky and provided light enough to see clearly. We came to a meadow a short distance from the lake where the Master finally stopped.

He waited while we got comfortable. He joked with us saying, "You guys really are in bad shape. You need to get out and hike more." When we had all gathered, he asked,

"Before I start, do you have any questions?"

There was a girl sitting somewhere behind me. I think her name was Sarah. She asked in a careful, quiet voice, "Master, why do I get so depressed? Sometimes I just get into this funk."

"There are many different reasons for depression but sometimes things happen that are out of our control," he explained. "Your closest friend dies, or something happens to your body, like that fellow in the wheelchair. Sometimes it's a state of mind that you get into. It's like finding a dark corner somewhere where you can feel safe. A place where you think the world won't hurt you. Pain is pain whether you're the guy living on the street or a college grad with your whole life ahead of you!" He leaned down and looked right at her and I had the distinct feeling that he was seeing something about her situation. "Ultimately sadness is a state of mind. Fortunately, in your case, it's something that you can take control of. Be brave. I know you are very sensitive and you are aware of the suffering of humanity. Be strong, because you need to be strong to deal with it. Yes it's going to hurt, but there's an exquisite quality to that pain. Perhaps you can use this experience to go beyond all pain and illusion.

"This world is filled with suffering. I propose that you, meaning all of you, choose the path of love. Love can dissolve all pain. It's a divine force. It's a state of mind. Love, hate, anger, envy and even humor are all states of mind. So remember that you can change your state of mind. Be fluid in your approach and eventually it can be as easy as changing channels on a TV.

"To help you better survive in this world and keep your balance, I also want to teach about power. How to see it and be aware of it as a force. How to harvest it, and how to use self-control and only use it for a positive outcome. In Karate, the first thing you learn is discipline. So when we learn about power, we'll learn discipline."

"Master?" I said, getting up my nerve to ask a question.

"Yes."

"How do you do the things you do? The miracles?"

"If you ever reach that point in your practice, I'll be there to guide you, so don't worry. For now, just practice your meditation. I'll be watching. I can do that, you know! Like Santa Claus." We all laughed. "So be good, for goodness sake!"

He looked around at everyone in the group. "The energy I give you when you're in my presence is for you to apply to your meditation practice. I know that in an empowered state, you are capable of seeing things that you wouldn't be able to otherwise. Use this for your spiritual development, not to impress your friends.

After meditating in The Master's presence, we would be filled with a blissful energy that would actually alter our perceptions. It could be felt by others. It's a great high and the others told me that it would last for weeks. I would find myself seeing things that I normally wouldn't see. While under this high, it was possible to see auras and it was also much easier to understand things about life. It was possible to see life with a great deal of clarity. That might be understanding about myself or seeing things from the past in a new perspective. When I came in contact with other people, I knew they could sense something. There was a power that radiated from my being. I could often see their thoughts and read their minds.

He went on to explain. "There's a kind of exchange that occurs quite naturally when you get involved with another person. Simply because of the dynamics; you having more energy than they do. You will lose some, in the exchange. People you are likely to meet right now will drain some of this vital energy from you. When you connect to someone the connection goes both ways. So I recommend that you keep it to yourselves and apply this energy to your meditations."

I heard Hanuman's voice. "Guruji?"

"Yes my friend." I noticed The Master always spoke to Hanuman with a certain respect that was reserved for Hanuman only.

"I'm not getting any younger. I'll be seventy-nine in another week. I think about dying quite a bit these days. I want to know what's going to happen. What can I do to prepare myself?"

"Don't worry. You will be well taken care of when the time comes. I have a special place prepared for you. But I think this is a good question for everyone. You don't know when you're going to die. Trevor almost left this world yesterday."

I was stunned to hear him say this. I didn't think Franklin had a minute to tell him about what had happened on the street.

"When you die, you don't really die! Nobody really dies. 'OK,' you say. What about my Aunt Agnes? She died ten years ago. She got hit by a train and dragged over thirty yards. Then buzzards swooped down and picked out her eyes." There was a combination of laughter and groaning. "Then ants came and cleaned off her bones. She looked pretty dead." More laughter. "About now, I'd have to agree with you. Chances are she didn't last beyond the initial impact. So how can I say that there's no death?" He waited, but no one said anything.

"You see, life never ends. Your soul goes on. Death is 'survivable'. You're all living proof. You've died thousands of times, and you don't look that bad, considering all that you've been through. You've been strangled, poisoned, stabbed, and fed to hungry lions, and you're still here.

"But where are you when you're not here, when you're not being you. After you've left the body and your memories have dissolved, what are you then? They don't teach that sort of thing in school.

"I highly recommend that you read 'The Tibetan Book of the Dead.' I believe it's available in English. Hanuman?" he asked, looking around, "You would know this."

"Yes, I have a copy " came Hanuman's voice. "It was translated by W.Y. Evens-Wentz."

"When you read it, you should keep in mind that The Tibetan Book of the Dead is not actually for the dead." There was a lot of laughter. "It is to study, as a reference guide, to prepare for the journey. I'm sure that name was adopted during the translation.

"The Buddhists believe in having compassion for all living beings. The ultimate expression of this is the natural transition that occurs when you realize or become self realized, when you become one with your own true nature. This is why the book is read out loud to the departed in Tibet.

"After death, consciousness lingers for as long as seven days. During this time, the body is still capable of hearing. The things you say at this time can have an influence on the person who has departed. This is when it's time to read the book. This is what it was written for. So I suppose you could say that the Book of the Dead actually is for the dead." There was some light laughter.

"Once passing from this world, it's important to recognize the luminosity which will then be present before you. It is the essence of your own mind. Your greater mind, your God-mind. It is your own true nature. Recognition of this will free you from the endless cycle of birth and death. Recognition and liberation are simultaneous. If you fail at this time to recognize your own true nature, you will become more fixed, more identified with life and the illusions of life.

Recognition isn't something that occurs from a thought; it is more the nature of your being, in a state of complete surrender.

There is no thought involved, there is no YOU left to think. Recognition must therefore come from the deepest level of your being. This is the only way. Take heart, it is possible to train your being over the course of a life time. Meditation is the answer.

"Don't bother clinging to your body, it will be gone forever, you will never know it again. There will never be a physical immortality. This is not the nature of this world, and I wouldn't want it. It would be like being stuck in a revolving door. The bliss of eternity awaits the adventurous spirit. So, let go and move on freely. Let go of all fear and trust eternity, you'll have nothing left to loose.

"Think of it as leaving on a long trip to an exotic, location and it's so wonderful that you're never going to return. You say goodbye to everyone you love and walk out the door. Don't pack any bags because you have to leave everything behind. Everything you will need; will be there for you.

It's good to write a will. Physically leave all of your belongings in order and itemize everything in your will and where you want it all to go. This will help you to free your mind of your attachments. When it's time to leave; you won't look back. You will be taking this journey, so see it as an adventure.

"Here in the West, there is little understanding of the states beyond this physical plane. You know only the senses. Because of this, you are unprepared for what lies just beyond this thin layer of illusion. You don't know your own nature. This will change. Some great souls have incarnated and are among us now.

"Death is your opportunity to enter into an enlightened state directly. Immediately upon dying, you have the opportunity to see your own nature. Remember: it is the essence of your own mind. Your mind, in Buddhist terms, is separate from all of the experiences that you think of as being 'you'. Your mind is the natural state from which all thought and illusion arises.

"After you've been dead for a week, if you fail to recognize your own true nature, you will experience the wrathful deities. They are frightening. They have fire in their eyes and carry human skulls as body armor. Consuming the whole of space, they appear inescapable. You must understand and recognize that these are only projections of your own consciousness. Avoid being afraid and confused. Recognize that the deities you see are illusions of your own mind. When you recognize this, they will go away.

"There is a time when the light of this world has faded and the light of the next world has not yet appeared. When you finally realize that your body is gone and will never return, you may try to cling to another body out of fear and attachment. Attachment to the tactile sensations of touch and feel and taste. Your own attachments will draw you to another incarnation. You must let go of all attachment and desire. Learn to take refuge in the light of your own true nature. The only reason why you are born again is because you choose to do so.

"This has happened to you countless times. You have not recognized your natural state. You cling to incarnation because it's better than wandering through the endless worlds. The bardos are all only transitory states. You're in a bardo right now! This life is just another transient state. If it seems real to you, well, so do all of the other transient states. When you exit this world, it's important to recognize your death; otherwise you may wander as a ghost in confusion and uncertainty.

"When in the bardo outside of this life, you are like a feather in the wind, experiencing your own consciousness seeking only rebirth to escape what has become an endless existence of suffering. Suffering is something that you have created through your own ignorance. You believe your emotional states are real all of your petty jealousies and angers. The pain is so great that you may feel desperate to incarnate. You look for a luminous essence, or in your desperation, you look for a body, any body. In your desperation you may take a lower birth, maybe as an animal.

"Remember that this same opportunity to awaken is available in each moment you are alive. Here, in this world, right now; you can avoid this ultimate reality. You can do something else. Just look around you, out on the street. You're ultimately only fooling yourselves. Death will surly come to remind you. You live in this reality in every moment, whether you are incarnate or not. So let go of all of your loves, desires, and your hates. They are all very transitory. Once they're gone, they'll never return to you. We live in a luminous continuity that has no ending and no beginning. Wake up and see the perfection of your own nature! All of the images, all of the things you associate with this life, are simply projections of your limited awareness and not your true nature.

"All of existence is some kind of a bardo state, even this life that you are so convinced is real. This is why it's important to be mindful. In every moment there lies the possibility of recognizing your own true nature. Look at every thought, look to the source. It's right there, it's been there all of the time. This is what the Buddha did. This is what the Buddha taught. This is what you can do!"

Chapter 16

Summer of Love Begins

I heard the question being asked, "What happens when we reincarnate?"

The Master pointed to his navel chakra. "The Taoists say that all life began from the tantien. This is where the seed of life is planted and takes root. In the beginning there is only one energy one life form. The sex is undecided by the body, however the soul's karma will usually incarnate as the same sex throughout your journey of incarnations. Sometimes there can be confusion about gender at this time if there is a karma to work out. Then from this one is born the unity of yin and the yang. One of these opposing forces will become dominate."

I was impressed at how comfortably he moved from one reference to the next, seamlessly blending Tibetan Buddhism, Hinduism, Zen and Taoism.

"Opposing forces of equal strength depend upon each other to create a balance. This balance is visible everywhere in nature. A tree is strong and sturdy. We use its wood to build a house. Yet when the wind blows, the tree can give way. It doesn't resist. It simply bends and sways with the breeze. In a river, you see water flowing around stones. It is in this way that we can see the Tao in nature.

"What we seek is to live in this way, to live in harmony and balance with nature. We seek to be aware that we are just another part of nature. Nothing more! So, be like the tree: flexible yet strong, firm in your beliefs yet open to new ideas. We seek to live in harmony with the natural universe. With the Tao.

"I was watching some surfers out there," he said pointing out towards the Pacific, that was only blocks away, "I noticed that they weren't surfing; they were just sitting on their boards and feeling the movement of the waves. Hours went by like this. They never even attempted to ride any waves. They were, in the moment, just meditating to the rhythm of the ocean. I think they were dolphins in a past life." There was some laughter.

"No, really. I think they were! This is the path they follow. It is being in harmony with nature. "They were instinctively drawn back to follow their previous karma.

"There is a Dharma for all of us to follow. It's that perfect wave. Follow it and it will take you to Nirvana.

"If you could only awaken from this dream, you would know all of the wonders of this perfect universe. It's sad for me to see you living in such darkness." Then he added with a Cheshire Cat grin, "I guess this doesn't really answer your question. Just meditate!"

"Master? What can I do to help create balance in my life? I feel like I need a technique." Sue asked.

"Focus on your Tantien. This is your center for balance. With each breathe; focus on drawing each breath from that point." He folded his hands on his lower belly and took a deep breath. "You'll breath in deeper. Another technique you can use is to get a small stone, a quartz crystal. You might remember; this is something we used in Atlantis. Get it mounted and hang it from a waist chain. Be sure the crystal is over your Tantien. When ever you feel it; it will remind you to focus there.

"Back in Atlantis these stones held more 'prana'. It was easier to feel their power. However, in today's world the energy we live in has becoming much too dense for the subtleties of the crystals to affect us; they mostly serve as decoration. But you can still use it as a reminder. Similar to a string tied to around your finger, whenever you feel it; you will be reminded."

We were all quiet for a few minutes. The Master stood in a meditative state. I could clearly see the presence of his aura; he looked magnificent. He barely seemed to be in this world. He stood absorbed in a motionless state of ecstacy for several minutes. I simply sat and watched the splender of his aura until he spoke again.

"One of the ways out of the karma that holds you here is through selfless giving. In the eyes of God, it is noble to eliminate the suffering of others. You can do this in every action you are engaged in, from feeding the poor to the way you smile at the person working behind the counter. It's all part of conscious living. Be present in every moment. It doesn't have to cost money, and it doesn't even have to take extra time. It's simply conscious living. Be aware of how you treat others in your every day life. Make that extra effort to be kind. This will actually make you feel better about yourself. Do it for selfish reasons if you have to. Eventually you'll stop thinking about yourself, and you'll do it for the joy it brings to others. Lose yourself in your giving, it will free you."

"But Master," Vajra implored, "I thought we were supposed to be detached from life. It seems like caring for everybody will just make us more attached."

"Lose yourself in your caring. Lose your attachment to yourself. Use this practice to lose your self; the self that thinks it cares or doesn't. God is everywhere, in every moment. It is impossible to detach yourself from this divine presence. To do so is to live in illusion. Walk down the street, and you'll see lots of people who are clearly detached from this truth. They live in illusion all the way to the grave and even beyond the grave. When you serve others, you serve God."

"Master," Vajra asked, "If God is here now, and if we are already God, then why are we not enlightened?"

"Because you still live in illusion."

He turned his back to us and in an obvious gesture, turning his head from side to side as if he was looking for something, then explained, "If you are not looking at it, then you simply won't see it." He turned again, this time facing us, and added, "It's only when you look directly at the truth, that you can see and understand it."

He then continued, "There are many layers of illusion that are wrapped around you. You need to be honest with yourselves and look beyond your illusions." He looked up at the sky, "When there are clouds, you can't see the stars. This doesn't mean they don't exist. Similarly, the truth is always present. Meditate deeply and you will be able to look beyond the clouds.

"Picture a piece of broken glass that's been sitting on the shore. At first it's edges are rough. You have to be very careful when you pick it up so you won't cut yourself. If you leave it long enough on the shore, the ocean eventually wears the edges smooth. Similarly, with your illusions, if you practice proper meditation and mindfulness, they will eventually dissolve into the great ocean of existence."

I looked up and gazed at the stars. Standing before us, The Master looked 'bigger than life'. He looked up at the night sky and very dramatically raised his hands, palms facing toward the stars, and said, "Look at the stars." He gracefully raised his right hand and moving it in a circular motion. "Just keep looking."

I looked upward toward the eastern sky and after a moment, I could see the stars begin to move all about. It looked like ten thousand shooting stars. It was a beautiful sight. I heard the Master's voice saying, "They're alive, and they're dancing just for you."

When I looked at him, he smiled and said, "You know, if you tell people this, no one will believe you. They'll say I gave you LSD or that I used hypnosis. So this is just for you. For you to witness and to keep close to your hearts.

"Solstice day has passed. Welcome a new beginning as we sit poised on the threshold of a new age.

"Remember to be kind to others. Treat people with dignity. Many of them have difficult lives and karmas. You don't necessarily have to invite them into your home," there was some laughter, "but always remember that you're not that different. You have different karma, but you're ultimately the same: flesh, blood, and bone. Whether you're born here or in Africa, you're all children of God. Only your self-delusion separates you.

"Tonight I did something unusual. I've been doing it for the past several years. I intervened. I've done this out of love. This isn't done very often, but the energy was right. Young people, in particular, are ready. They're ready for a change. For the past few years, there's been a very brave movement here, in this country. A movement for civil rights and equality. I want this to succeed. This is something that is long overdue.

The fact that it is necessarily to fight for basic equality, suggest a need to evolve spiritually. Let's see if humanity gets this simple truth. We are all equal. Any differences you perceive are born out of ignorance."

"Master?" Franklin asked.

"Yes Ganesha." The Master said as he pointed at Franklin. Ganesha must be the name he was given during the initiation.

"What's going to happen now? Is there going to be peace on Earth?"

"We have to wait and see. It's up to mankind." He looked ponderous, shuffling about while casting his gaze to the ground. "This is a warning to the world. If we don't change the way we do things..." He stopped and put his hand over his forehead in a very dramatic gesture, like he suddenly had a migraine. The Master was silent.

Sue called out, "Guruji, are you alright?"

He dropped his hand and said, "I just saw an earthquake here in San Francisco. The city will one day be completely destroyed."

"When?" everyone shouted at once.

"Don't worry. It's not for many years. There will be warnings for those who are sensitive and can read the signs."

The others kept pressing him for a date, but he ignored their pleadings. He seemed preoccupied with his current thought. I really don't know why, but I felt it was inappropriate to press with further questions. I felt content with his answer.

He continued. "If things don't change, there will be repercussions. This isn't my choice it's karma. As you know, we're at the end of the Kali Yuga. If you're not familiar with the Goddess Kali, she is known as the bringer of destruction. On a personal level, she will destroy all of your attachments and your illusions. She does this by taking things from you that you love and cherish most. This can be a very painful process. The more you try to hold on to your illusions, the more painful it will be.

On a global level, she will bring about the end of this age through destruction. So cling to nothing!

I see a catastrophe looming. The imbalance is in the ethereal and it will soon manifest if there is no change. By looming, I mean as soon as forty to fifty years from this time. Sometimes karma takes a while to manifest. Right now you may think this is a long time away. But it will come. Your lives will go by faster than you think. So enjoy this time we now share, because it won't last.

"Two thousand years ago, mankind took the life of an Enlightened being. All of the people responsible for that act are long gone, they've incarnated in this world over and over again. Their souls and the karma for their actions remain. Part of the karma is theirs alone to suffer, but some of it lies with all of humanity. This never could have happened in India. But the Western world lives in such darkness. You see, this same thing would have happened almost anywhere in the West, it's symptomatic of degenerating human consciousness. There's very little respect for the teaching of enlightenment in this world.

"Humankind will have to change or suffer the consequences. There are different cycles of karma some are instant; some, the greater karmas, take much longer. That which I see looming is a part of a greater karma. I see cities being destroyed"

Terra was Italian born and still had family living in Italy. With concerned about her family she asked, "What will happen to Rome?"

"I see it being destroyed. Rome itself will not survive. I see the city in a blaze, reduced to ashes. It's not the only city that will perish. I see many events in the future that will change the shape of the world, both geographically and politically. You can expect this all to occur within forty to seventy five years from this time.

"The Earth is ill. I see nature being violated, and she will react violently! Expect to see earthquakes greater than anything in human memory. The land we are standing on will lie under water. These things won't happen soon, but I see it happening. There will be signs. The ice on the Earth's polar caps will begin to melt and leave vast areas of land under water. Before this occurs I see the beginnings of war. Shortly after the natural world will begin to purge.

"You see, life is out of balance. Nature will react. We need to be stewards of this planet, not exploiters. If we don't begin very soon, There will be very serious problems for all of humanity.

"The teachings of enlightenment should be available for all. It's important for people to hear the truth. From this time on, there will be many spiritual teachers coming to America. Be discriminating about who you choose to study with. Look beyond the words, use your intuition and you'll know. If you choose not to continue the study of enlightenment, that's OK. I will respect your decision; just never get in the way of anyone else's dharma. This is one of the worst kinds of karma.

"I want you to wait before telling your story. When the time is right; you should tell the world. Look for me when the time comes. I'll guide you.

"So, if you choose to go out and spread the dharma; you have my blessing. It will be easiest to for the next thirty-five to forty-five years; the door will close shortly after that. Anyone who seeks the truth will have to come to you."

The Master was speaking in stream of consciousness, he started pacing, with a concerned expression, like he was far away, barely paying attention to us. "I see that there could be a major war starting within the the next forty to fifty years. A World War." He stopped and looked right at us, one by one. "Time passes much faster than you think. Many of you will live to see the beginning of this war.

"Time is relative. From my point of view, a life time is like a blink of an eye. Your lives will be over before you know it. Right now this sounds like it's far away in some Orwellian future. I assure you, many of you will live to see it!"

"Will there be a Third World War, and who will start it?" Vajra asked.

"It will come from the Middle East. It will come suddenly and shock the world. There will be no negotiation. It may start as an act of terrorism. But I eventually see an invasion of southern Europe. Spain, Italy, and France will all fall. They'll be taken by surprise. America will not be invaded, but will suffer attacks."

Vajra seemed incredulous, "But we've got the bomb! They'd be crazy to start a war with us!"

"They'll have it too. Southern Russia will fall, along with its nuclear arsenal and its secrets.

"America will be reluctant to uses the these types of weapons, knowing there will be a cloud of nuclear dust and radiation that will darken the skies throughout the Earth. However, I don't see just one bomb being used; there are likely to be several. This is what I see happening to several European and Middle Eastern cities. What I see are images of possible futures. I see cities laid to ashes, I can only interpret the images from these visions.

"Visions are only possible futures. Things don't necessarily have to be this way. Yet if there are not substantial changes in human consciousness, it will surely come to pass. It's like changing the course of a river. It will take effort, but it can be done.

"On a deeper level it has to do with man's relationship to that divine presence we call God. It is necessary to change the hearts and minds of humankind.

"I see the world rushing headlong into disaster. We are violating the most basic laws of nature and the events of the future are only a response to the human consciousness. We are out of balance. Nations will fight over false religions and eventually over dwindling resources. A great drought will come, caused by war and neglect to our planet. Be forewarned: these things I see will come to pass if humankind doesn't change."

I asked one more question, "How long will this war last?"

"This war will not end for many, many years. I see a generation being born under this cloud. It will last for over a quarter of a century. This will be the last world war. If we don't accept the value of love now, then perhaps we then will see the inherent wisdom of this philosophy. Humanity has a collective consciousness that is unbroken through time. This is how it is that we share the greater karmas.

"It is in times of our greatest adversities that we find our greatest strengths and virtues. Use what life brings you. Always aspire to the noblest of all truths. God is everywhere. Present in all of creation. Darkness is always followed by light.

"Know that I love you and will be there to guide you when you leave this transitory world. I am forever with you."

There were many more predictions he made that evening. Many that seemed impossible at that time but have all come true; others are still off in the possible future. He told us that eventually a great age of peace would come. I've learned over the years that we really do hold the future in our hands. But so far everything The Master predicted that evening and on other occasions have in fact come true. Sometimes the dates were off, but not by much.

He spoke until sunrise, telling us not to fear the Soviet Union and predicted its eventual fall. He also predicted the coming of the computer age; he said it would eventually touch every part of our lives. He was right about everything! Yet he said that it is the collective consciousness of all people that will ultimately decide our fate.

The Master finished speaking then sat in a state of complete silence. The colors of the sunrise were changing the sky. I sat as a whitness and watched as he passed into a state of bliss. He was beautifully majestic. His skin had a shine to it that was otherworldly. I gazed in awe as his body slowly faded from view. Within minutes, he was completely gone from this world.

I've tried to tell you my story just as it was written in my notes and as I can best remember it, changing only the names of the people who were there to protect their privacy.

For a very brief time there was a portal between the worlds, bringing a feeling of hope and a message of love to us all. After waiting for over thirty years it has been my privilege to finally tell you this remarkable story.

It is my eternal hope that this brings some inspiration and light into your lives. The Summer of Love is always present, always here. Look just beyond the illusion of time.

May we all awaken from the Dream!

Acknowledgments

*I would like to thank my wife Una
for her love, kindness and support.
Without her suggestions and the countless hours of
editing this would not be possible.
I would also thank Tom Skelly for his artistic
skill and vision in producing such as wonderful cover design.
I am grateful to Bob Reed for his positive support of this project and
dedicated effort in getting this book to you.
I would like to thank all of the teachers
throught my life that helped me along my journey.*